To Billy,

Watch ou

Regards,

E. Blood

(aka)

The House on Creep Street

A Fright Friends Adventure

By

The Blood Brothers

www.AuthorMikeInk.com

ISBN: 9780991033003
Library of Congress Control Number: 2014931598

First Published by *AuthorMike Spooky Ink*, 9/1/2014

www.AuthorMikeInk.com

AuthorMike Spooky Ink and its logo are trademarked by *AuthorMike Ink Publishing*.

Printed in the United States of America

In Memory of Lou Evangelista.

"The rest is history."

"Understand death? Sure. That was when the monsters got you."

-Stephen King, *Salem's Lot*

PROLOGUE

There is a legend in the small, tree-lined town of Blackwood.

Have you heard it?

Like most small towns, Blackwood hides its secrets away like a virus, hoping its contagions will not hitch the wind over the surrounding green hills to the neighboring communities beyond. Only the older citizens of Blackwood know of the big spooky house perched on its isolated street and of the night-drenched murder that took place there decades ago. For years, this Blackwood house has stood unoccupied. Nothing dared live within its creaking and rotting walls. It was said that even rats and low, scurrying insects would avoid the ancient structure.

And like most small towns, old and creepy houses also have stories—of blood-curdling screams, and headless specters, and clanking chains. And the longer these houses exist, the more detailed their stories become—as if they were something organic. Alive. The line between neighborhood folklore and reality becomes increasingly blurred until it vanishes entirely. The legends of houses like these grow as their weed-infested gardens grow. And lying at the bottom of their black earth will always be the root.

When it comes to things that go bump in the night on Creep Street, the small-minded adults of the town may claim nonsense and blame their children's overactive imaginations on their consumption of monster movies and ghastly comic books, but it doesn't make the legend any less real. And the legend of Blackwood's haunted house remains firmly entrenched in the small town's history. Told and retold by the curious and the fascinated and the terrified, the story of Halloween murder, and of innocence reborn into monstrousness, remains an urban myth that refuses to die.

Much like the lone inhabitant of the house on Creep Street.

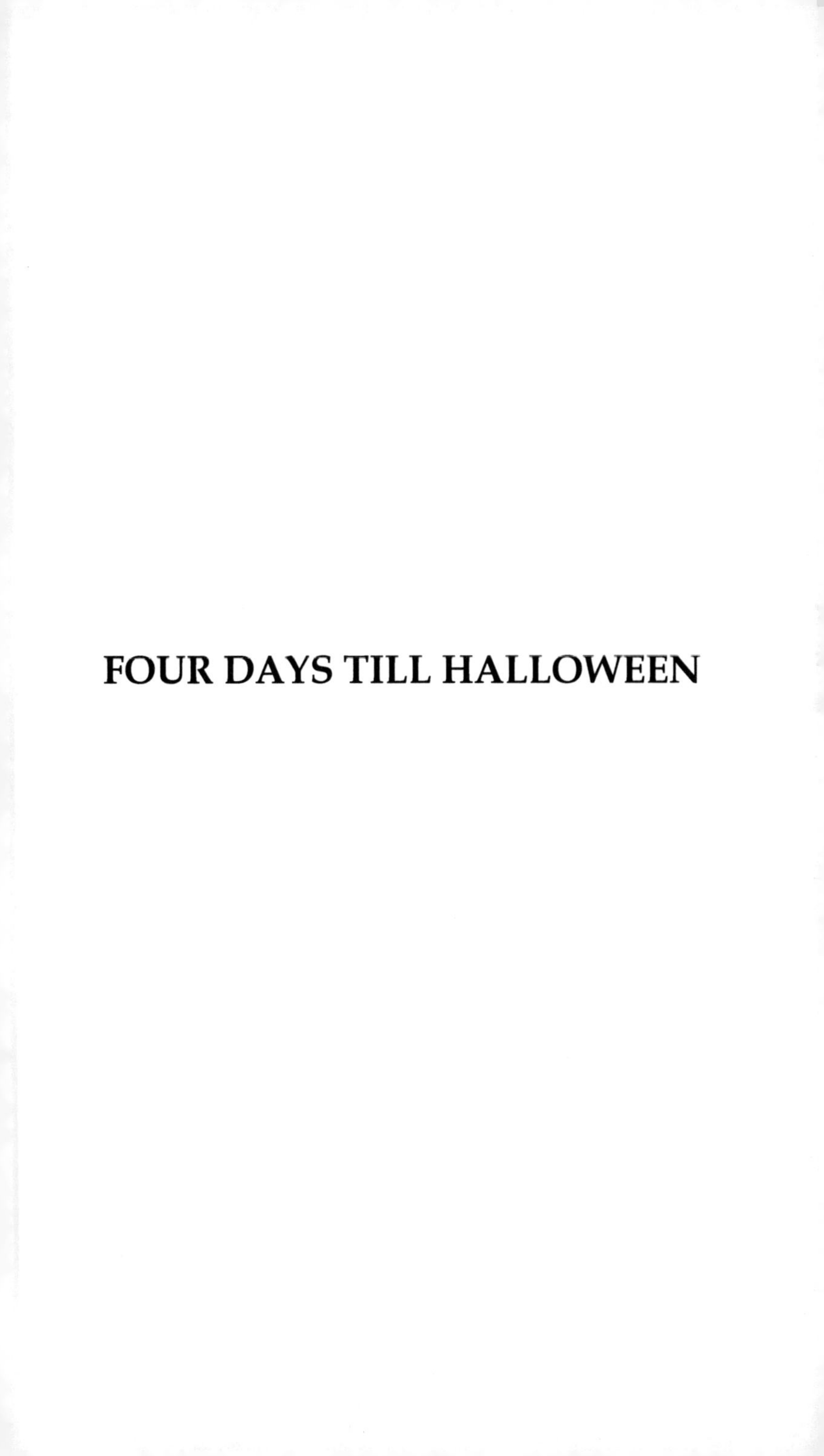

FOUR DAYS TILL HALLOWEEN

CHAPTER 1

An early autumn night had just begun to fall as Joey Tonelli stared into the black eyeholes of the bleached and bony skull. It sat before him and grinned an evil grin, its white teeth stained with blood. A slimy snake crawled inside one eyehole and out the other as a monstrous spider rested on the very top of the empty head. Just when Joey thought he could hear the soft hiss of the snake and the prickly hair of the spider's legs, he was snapped back to reality by the voice just behind him.

"I'm done with trick-or-treating, dude. It's for little kids."

Joey continued to stare at the skull, which he imagined grinning wider and wider until its dry bone shattered. Then he sighed.

The skull was just one of many masks and costumes in the main display window of Irwin's Hardware. Inside the window sat clattering skeletons, deranged witches, and scary vampires with gory fangs. They all stared back at Joey from their many rows, surrounded by fake cobwebs, black candles, and orange crepe paper.

The greatest night of the year was almost here.

October 31st.

Halloween.

But like some cruel joke from the universe, Joey's two best friends, Kevin and Barry, didn't seem to have interest in trick-or-treating any longer. All three boys were only twelve years old, and while Kevin and Barry were slowly maturing day by day, Joey seemingly refused to. He was still obsessed with monster toys, and horror comic books, and the eternal pursuit of the perfect Halloween costume.

"How can you guys say Halloween is just for little kids?" Joey demanded, finally turning to face his friends.

Kevin rolled his eyes. "Joey, c'mon," he began. "Another year of dressing like a ghost, or a robot? We're getting too old for that stuff."

Joey couldn't help but glare at his friend Kevin, who had changed a lot in the last year. Recently, Kevin had discovered he was something of a hot item around the halls of Mary Shelley Middle School. The girls would bat their eyes and giggle nervously as he walked by, and he loved every minute of it. He felt like he was finally becoming a "real man," so he didn't have time to dress up like a monster and go begging for candy.

Joey turned with pleading eyes to Barry, who had always been the more easygoing member of the group.

"Come on, back me up," he begged his friend. "*You* still wanna go trick-or-treating, right?"

Barry, who had been best friends with both Joey and Kevin since their first day of elementary school, glanced at his shoes. He was ashamed of upsetting his friend for the sake of going along with Kevin in order to feel older—and cooler. Barry, who was heavier than most boys his age (a fact that never ceased to cause him internal embarrassment), had all the time in the world to go begging for candy. And the last thing he wanted to do was hurt Joey's feelings. But if he had to choose sides, he would have to choose Kevin. As rotten and lame as it made him feel, he had to admit that Kevin was officially the "cool one" of the group—and that was all Barry ever wanted to be.

Always the peacekeeper, however, his eyes went wide in excitement.

"There'll be some *great* spooky movies airing on Halloween night!" he said with forced enthusiasm. "We can all go to my house, and we'll make popcorn and cheesy nachos and watch them all! It'll be great!"

Kevin laughed and patted Barry's belly. "Do you really have room in there for *more* nachos?"

Barry's face warmed over and he fought the frown tugging at his cheeks.

Joey, feeling even more alone in this conversation, crossed his arms. "So you're out, too? Since when are you too old for free food, Barry?"

Kevin laughed out loud at Joey's joke, but thought better of high-fiving him, considering Joey was really sore at him at that moment.

Barry did not think either friend's joke was particularly funny, as he didn't like it when they made fun of his weight. In fact, he would say he downright hated it. But he was not the type of kid who was good at sticking up for himself. It was much easier to laugh along with the jokes, and so he laughed along with them now, hoping to lighten the mood.

The darkening evening caused Joey to check his watch and he saw that it was almost six o'clock. The night winds were suddenly fierce, but it was that perfect time of year when it wasn't too warm or too cold. Leaves fell from tree branches and showered the ground. Houses were plastered with Halloween decorations. Every window contained a vampire or mummy face, whose dark eyes loomed on those who passed by. Dummies sat on porches, their straw-filled bodies dressed in flannel shirts. Illuminated eyes of jack-o-lanterns sat on porch railings and glowed in the night.

Joey stared at his Halloween surroundings and realized with bitterness that people of all ages—and much older than Barry and Kevin—respected Halloween enough to at least decorate their houses and carve some lousy pumpkins. And Joey was sure that after these people had finished their decorating and carving, they all had gone down to Blackwood General and purchased bag after bag of candy for all the trick-or-treaters that would soon be invading their front porches.

So why was it that Joey found himself stuck with the only two kids in all of Blackwood who no longer felt Halloween was worth celebrating? He could feel anger building slowly within him again, and though he tried to ignore it, the frustration began to spill.

"It's stupid to say we're too old to trick-or-treat. Who cares if we're twelve?" Joey demanded, shoving his hands into the pockets of his black denim jacket. He could sense that his outburst was bordering on tantrum, but this wasn't any old day of the year they were talking about, here. It was Halloween! "I even know kids in *high school* who still go trick-or-treating!" he lied.

"Like who?" Kevin challenged.

Joey thought for a moment, desperately searching his mind for the many names of kids that attended high school. Scott DeForrest? Peter Reeves, maybe? Surely he could think of *someone*!

"I know!" Joey proudly exclaimed. "Douglas! You know, Mario's friend!"

"Your brother doesn't have any friends!" Kevin laughed.

"Wasn't Douglas that kid who set the boys' bathroom trashcan on fire one day when he was sneaking a smoke?" asked Barry, skeptically. Kevin laughed again, and the two boys high-fived. Joey, however, was not amused. He turned away from his friends and looked back into the storefront window, admiring the masks on the middle shelf.

"Halloween is kid stuff. Why is it such a big deal to you?" Kevin asked Joey, who continued to stare at Mr. Irwin's collection of masks. Joey was about to answer when he saw Kevin's reflection in the windowpane—and caught him rolling his eyes to Barry.

"Because it is!" Joey firmly answered, spinning to face his friends again. "Because if we don't trick-or-treat, or stay up all night making prank phone calls, or fill Carl Arven's mailbox with shaving cream, then we have to actually grow up! We have to grow up and get jobs and pay bills and everything else that comes with getting older!"

Neither friend spoke.

Joey eyed Barry harshly. "Are you looking forward to that?" he asked, and Barry shook his head. "How about you, Kevin?" Joey asked. "Are you looking forward to overtime and taxes and mowing the lawn every day?"

"My dad doesn't mow the lawn every day!" Kevin argued back, but he could see his argument was useless.

Joey was stubborn in general—it was just part of his personality. He certainly didn't demand that things *always* be his way, but there were certain things he felt strongly about—even if his friends didn't. And he would admit that sometimes the stuff he valued was a little cornball and silly, but not this. Not Halloween. His friends could refuse to trick-or-treat all they wanted, but Joey would die before admitting it wasn't important—that it was merely...*kid stuff.*

Kevin could see the disappointment in Joey's face, so he finally softened and put an arm around his friend's shoulder. "Come on, dude, we'll be late for the movie," he said and led Joey away from the storefront window.

As the boys walked down to Main Street Theater to catch their horror double bill of *Clown Town* and *Count Rockwood: The Old-Fashioned Vampire,* autumn leaves blew carelessly all around them, ushering in another Halloween—one that Joey Tonelli would apparently be celebrating alone.

CHAPTER TWO

At any other time of year, Main Street Theater was deserted. People did not have much use for an old, single-screen movie house when they could travel to the nearby bustling city of Bradbury and attend the Googolplex, which had ear-shattering surround sound and eyeball-watering 3D. Despite this, Main Street Theater had managed to stay in business, and it was especially popular during the month of October, when it ran classic (and not-so-classic) horror films on weekends.

Joey, Kevin, and Barry took their seats in the busy theater for the double bill, which was scheduled to begin at six o'clock. Barry had two large tubs of popcorn cradled in his arms, and Kevin carried his friend's mega-jumbo soda for him.

Joey was in a dark mood. The very thought of skipping trick-or-treating that year was gnawing at his brain like a jackal picking at a piece of road kill.

I guess I'll be trick-or-treating alone, he thought glumly, before scolding himself. *Who goes trick-or-treating alone? A loser, that's who.*

"Any babes in here?" Kevin grinned, taking off his lucky blue ball cap. He smoothed down his parted black hair, as if this very act would cause any girl in the theater to fling herself at him.

As Barry began chomping down on fistfuls of his extra-buttery popcorn, Joey slumped in his seat and sighed, balling his hand into a fist and resting his head against it.

The first movie began playing, and the audience of mostly teens and pre-teens went wild—hooting and hollering and throwing their candy snacks in the air.

Joey's mind drifted.

I've gotta think of a way to get the dudes interested in Halloween again…but how…?

As he watched a group of teenagers in letter jackets and cheerleader outfits enter the old, abandoned house on the big silver screen, Joey was hit with sudden inspiration. Images of that lone, creepy house in the corner of Blackwood suddenly sprang up in his mind. He pictured its ancient design and dead, groaning wood, and his imagination concocted tattered curtains swaying in windows with evil eyes glowing just behind them; and perhaps there were screams—maybe a young woman's as she confronted the unseen terrors that dwelled within the eerie house's walls.

Every small town has at least one house the children whisper about; the type of house that has always been abandoned; where the once pristine white paint has faded to a grimy gray; where the windows are boarded, and the lawn never grows; where children hold their breath and close their eyes as they pass by.

A house that sounds like it contains an army of whispering spirits when the wind whistles through the nearby trees.

In the town of Blackwood, that house could be found on Creep Street. It had stood there as long as he could remember.

That's it! Joey thought excitedly. *I'll get Kevin and Barry back into the Halloween spirit by bringing them to the house on Creep Street!* He celebrated inside his mind, already confident his plan would work. He eagerly looked over to his two friends, who watched the movie with looks of amusement on their faces. Joey hoped both flicks would fly right by. There was much to do that night.

This has gotta work! Joey thought to himself, feeling rejuvenated. *I'll show them spooky stuff can still be fun, even if I have to push them through the front door of that old place myself!*

* * *

After the double feature ended, the three friends left the theater. Kevin and Barry laughed and quoted terrible lines from both movies.

"'Your neck is perfect for my fangs!'" Kevin laughed in a faux vampire accent.

"'Oh my gosh, these custard pies are filled with BRAINS!'" Barry gleefully shouted.

"Hey guys, wanna go somewhere fun?" Joey interrupted, sipping the last of his soda before chucking it at a nearby trashcan. The soda can hit the rim and fell onto the street, clanking away down the block, carried by the autumn wind.

"Go to Chicken Lickens?" Barry asked, his face lighting up at the mention of his favorite fast-food joint.

"Jeeze, Barry, do you have that place on speed dial?" Joey muttered, causing his previously excited friend to frown.

"I know where we can go!" Kevin said through a grin. "We can go spy on Barry's foxy sister!"

Barry punched him on the arm.

"We're going," Joey said, pausing for dramatic emphasis, "to Creep Street!"

A nervous look settled on both Kevin and Barry's faces.

"That is…unless you guys are too scared?" Joey teased, stuffing his hands into the pockets of his jeans. He knew that was all he had to say to seal the deal. Kevin's face quickly hardened at the challenge, and Barry sighed, knowing he had no choice but to follow along—or be called a chicken for the rest of his life.

Creep Street was at the very edge of town and intersected the road on which both Joey and Barry lived—King Street. As the boys walked past both of their houses, Barry stared longingly at his own, wanting nothing more than to go inside, lock the door behind him, and not even *think* of going anywhere near the house on Creep Street.

"You s-sure we shouldn't just go home?" he asked, nervously, his eyes still on his house.

"Where's your sense of adventure, Barry?" Joey exclaimed, walking in front of his two friends. He kicked a can down the street. The sound echoed off the cool fall air.

As the boys approached, they could see the house waiting in the distance. Even from afar, it had the power to chill their bones. It was the sole remaining structure on the otherwise barren street—the other houses had been torn down years ago to make way for a real estate deal that never happened. Three stories tall and built in a Victorian style, it stood at the end of the block and loomed above the landscape—pitch-black, and composed of uneven angles and jutting arches. A single dead sycamore tree stood by the house, its twisted bare branches reaching out like the arms of a deformed spider.

As the three boys stood on the dead lawn looking up at the cold, blank face of the house, it was easy for them to understand why every kid in Blackwood believed it was haunted. The place was beyond creepy, and though it was likely Joey's imagination, he could've sworn he heard the house's old wood creaking and cracking, as if it were breathing...

He was beginning to have second thoughts. Even to him—a boy obsessed with all things creepy—the house was unnaturally eerie. Being in its very presence gave him gooseflesh.

"Now what?" Kevin asked, his arms crossed. Joey could tell that Kevin was trying hard to act like he didn't have the willies, but he wasn't doing a very good job.

"We go in," Joey answered. Though he was looking up at the house, he knew his friends' mouths had gone wide in shock. He smiled in response, confident in his plan.

A chilly wind blew, and the dead sycamore tree shook violently, sending chips of bark hurtling to the ground. Almost on instinct, Joey checked his watch. He saw it was almost ten o'clock. If he was out much later, his parents were going to hit the roof, and his father would probably threaten to throw away all of his rare, out-of-print VHS horror tapes—which was the go-to intimidation of choice for the old man.

But this was too important. Halloween was at stake.

Joey was just about to ask his friends who would be the first to go inside.

Then he saw a pale, hollow-eyed face in the upstairs window…and it was looking right at them.

CHAPTER THREE

Joey gasped and took a step back. "Dudes, look!" he shouted, and pointed to the window where the face had been. It was dark now, and the curtain around the window inside the house looked still and undisturbed.

"What is it?" asked Barry, digging into the pockets of his jeans and retrieving leftover movie candy.

"I saw a face in that window!" Joey insisted. He spun and looked at each of his friends. "Tell me *one* of you saw it!"

Kevin furrowed his brow at his friend and looked at the window again. "I didn't see anything. What was it?"

"A face!" Joey repeated, frustrated. "A face in that upstairs window! It was looking at us! I think it was a ghost!"

Barry tossed some candies into his mouth and then poured some into Kevin's waiting hand before extending the open bag to Joey. "Some candy?" he offered.

"I'm not making it up!" Joey yelled, swatting at Barry's hand and sending the candy scattering.

"My candy!" Barry cried out.

"Joey, we're not gonna fall for this," Kevin began. "And if you really think you saw something, it was probably because of the spooky flicks we just watched—especially that one about the ghost who stared out windows."

"Are you calling me a liar?" Joey demanded, staring hard into Kevin's face.

"I only said—"

Joey spun quickly on his heels, and without a moment's hesitation, began marching to the front door of the abandoned house.

"Is he going where I think he's going?" Barry asked Kevin, cocking his thumb at Joey's back.

"Joey, have you gone bananas?" Kevin called after his friend.

Joey could hear real concern in Kevin's voice, but he didn't care, and he didn't slow down…even as the very first step of the rickety porch noticeably squealed in protest under his feet.

"Don't you go in there!" Barry demanded.

Joey grasped the knob of the front door, finding it uncannily cold to the touch. The door was unlocked and it opened with an eerie squeal. He hesitated for a moment, peering into the dark mustiness of the house. Considering the possibility that this was, in fact, a *bad* idea, he turned back to his friends, who stood like statues on the sidewalk.

He remembered their disbelief and their sarcastic comments.

He pictured Kevin's sneer as he cracked his jokes.

Joey turned and stepped into the house on Creep Street, letting the darkness surround him until he vanished from the sight of his two friends.

The house reeked of many abandoned decades; of water-damaged wood and stale air; of dust and decay. It took a moment for his eyes to adjust to the dark before he could barely make out the lumpy shapes in the gloom all around him. The shapes seemed to throb and pulsate, as if each were alive. It was only when his eyes further adjusted that he realized what he was seeing: furniture—perfectly normal tables, chairs, sofas; an ancient radio was parked in the corner of the room.

Joey pictured a ghost, or ghosts, hiding behind each stick of furniture, ready to leap out and scare him to death.

He chided himself before moving on.

Crooked photos hung on the wall, and he peered at each of them, as if he were admiring artwork in a museum. One of the photos depicted three people: a man and woman—both somewhat young—and a child. Joey leaned in close to the picture and examined the child, who was a young boy. He wore denim overalls over a striped shirt, and his hair was parted in the middle.

Joey carefully took the framed photo off the wall and examined the back. On the bottom left corner was small and pretty handwriting:

The Smahs
Bennington, Betty, & Bobby
1943

"The Smahs…?" Joey asked himself, but a noise from upstairs caught his attention.

"Joey!" a voice called, and he quickly spun to see Kevin and Barry standing at the front doorway.

"You guys just about gave me a heart attack!" Joey shouted, relieved to see his friends.

"What are you doing in here?" asked Barry, nervously eyeing the interior of the house.

"Yeah, find any ghosts?" Kevin sneered, still trying to sound brave.

Another noise from upstairs—this one far louder than the first—caught all of the boys' attention.

"What was that?" asked Kevin, and Joey peered at the winding staircase just before them. It seemed to be inviting them deeper into the house.

Though his heart was pounding furiously in his chest, Joey forced himself to be brave. He had been the one to enter this house, after all. And he *had* seen a face.

He placed the family photograph down and began slowly climbing the staircase, the wood beneath him groaning with each footfall.

"Joey, let's just get out of here," Barry pleaded. "Those steps might not even hold you!"

"They definitely wouldn't hol—" Kevin began, but another noise from upstairs interrupted his joke.

A door had slammed shut.

Joey's body iced over, as if he had just been thrown into the cold waters of a river in the dead of winter. But he didn't stop climbing, either.

"Joey, fine, whatever; you were right, I was wrong," said Kevin, finally showing his fear. "This house is filled with haunted faces and ghosts and the Wolf Man, and oh look, there's Mummy, how terrifying! There, I said it. Now can we just get out of here?"

"No way," said Joey, his shaking voice defying his own attempt to seem brave. "I gotta see what's making that noise."

"Joey, please..." Barry whimpered.

Joey ignored him and continued up the stairs until arriving at the top. He looked in both directions down the hallway, unsure where to go. Each hallway stretched off into the blackness, and both were almost mirror images of each other. Down each corridor were several doors—all of them closed tight.

Scratching sounds now filled the darkness and seemed to be originating from behind one of the closed doors...but which one?

Joey stepped off the staircase and began walking slowly down the hallway to his left. He tiptoed, his sneakers sinking into the plush carpet under him. The sounds had stopped, but his sights were set on the far door at the end of the hallway.

As he crept closer, the door opened with a shrill squeal. He stopped in his tracks, his heart beating so frantically he thought it might burst from his chest.

A pale white hand stuck out of the darkness of the door crack and beckoned him closer with a single sickly finger.

"I've been waiting for someone…*anyone*…to visit," said a ghostly, whispering voice—pure menace lurked beneath the words.

Joey gasped, turning quickly to make his retreat back down the hallway…when he saw the monstrous creature standing before him. Its mouth was full of razor-sharp teeth, and its matted black hair covered parts of its scabbed and scarred and scaly flesh.

Joey shrieked as the creature grabbed him in the darkness.

CHAPTER FOUR

The hideous creature began to laugh, even as Joey easily wriggled free from its clutches. It was not a malicious laugh—rather, it was one of pure glee. And a little muffled.

Joey stopped screaming as it dawned on him that the creature was wearing a mask.

"What...?" he gasped.

The "creature" pulled off its mask and revealed the face of Mario, Joey's older brother.

"Oh, you've gotta be kidding," Joey said, glaring at his laughing sibling.

Kevin and Barry came bounding up the stairs.

"We'll save you, Joey!" Barry was yelling. "Well, Kevin will save you, and I'll cheer for him!"

Mario began laughing even harder. When Kevin and Barry saw him, they both gasped.

"Mario the Man!" Barry whispered.

Both of Joey's friends were in awe of Mario, even though he was relentlessly mean to them. They knew in their middle school hearts that Mario was the cool kid they would never be.

"Holy cow, you should've seen your face, Joey!" Mario laughed, clutching the rubber monster mask to his chest. "You looked like an ape!"

"Shut up, Mario!" Joey said angrily. His fear was slowly fading, even as his heart continued to pound in his chest.

"H-hi, Mario," Kevin said awkwardly.

"Shut up, dweeb," Mario said without even looking at him.

"What are you doing here?" Joey demanded.

"Mom sent me out to find you because you're out past curfew, idiot," Mario said. "And I saw you three dorks come in here, so I snuck in through the back door. You're so lame that I walked up those steps right behind you and you didn't even notice!"

"You nearly made my skeleton jump out of my skin," Joey said, his hand to his heart. "How did you make that creepy hand appear in that doorway?"

The look of glee slowly faded from Mario's face and he raised an eyebrow. "Uh…what hand?"

"The white hand," Joey said. "The one that came out of that door." He pointed to the doorway behind them where he had witnessed the hand creep out of the darkness.

Mario looked at Joey, and then at Kevin and Barry, who only shrugged. "Nice try, Joey," he finally said, turning back to his brother. "C'mon, let's go home. Dad is gonna pitch a fit if he knows you were out this late."

"No, wait a second!" Joey said. "The hand and the whispering voice? The face in the upstairs window? That wasn't you?"

"What are you talking about? What face?" Mario asked, sounding bored. He wasn't even looking at Joey anymore, but instead was fiddling with a loose fang on his rubber mask. "Let's go, man. I told Douglas I'd meet him at the diner."

"Guys, did *you* see the hand?" Joey asked desperately to his friends. "Did you hear the voice?"

Barry looked ashamed. "Well…we were still downstairs."

"Yeah," Kevin grinned. "Barry was busy wetting himself."

"I did NOT wet myself—I popped my barrel juice!" Barry protested.

"Whatever, let's go!" Mario said.

The boys each walked down the stairs and out the front door.

Outside, the chilly wind still blew. On every other doorstep of every other house sat a grinning jack-o-lantern, the burning candles within flickering against that autumn wind. Their leering faces all seemed to be fixed on Joey, who had a sick and uneasy feeling. Their walk home was quiet, filled only with the sounds of the night.

They reached Barry's house first. He waved goodbye and walked inside. Joey and Mario's house was next.

"Kevin, you gotta believe me," Joey said before parting ways with Kevin, who lived on the other side of town—the wealthier side. "I saw something in that house!"

"Joey, it was just your brother," Kevin said, not unkindly. "It's okay you got scared. We were all scared. Especially Barry. Man, you should've seen his face; it was—"

"Kevin, I'm serious!"

"I gotta go," Kevin said. "I'll see you tomorrow." And with that, he jogged off down the street.

Joey watched him for a moment until Mario gabbed him by his jacket sleeve and yanked him toward their own house.

Inside, Joey's mom sat at the kitchen table listening to a Dean Martin record and reading a book.

"Here, I brought the doofus home," Mario said, finally letting go of Joey's jacket sleeve. "I'm outta here."

"Don't be too late!" Mom said cheerfully.

Mario left without reply.

The kitchen was warm from the oven, and Joey could smell the heavenly aroma of the homemade pumpkin pie Mom was baking. She baked at all hours of the day, and sometimes well into the night. He always found it funny that she so easily fit the stereotype of the sweet and pleasant mother, who cited baking, reading romance novels, and listening to music from another era as her favorite hobbies.

"And where were you, young man?" Mom asked playfully. She wasn't really mad—nothing made Joey's mother really mad. She was the most cheerful person he knew.

"The movies," Joey said.

"What did you see?"

"Oh, some kid's cartoon," Joey lied, embarrassed to even say the titles of the films out loud.

Thoughts of what he had seen in the house on Creep Street suddenly drifted back into his mind, and he considered telling his mother—about the ghost he was convinced he had seen. One look at her smiling face told him there was no way she would believe him. But he had to tell *someone*.

"Where's Dad?" Joey asked.

"In the basement," Mom said, returning to her book. "The plumbing is acting up again."

Joey went down into the furnished basement, which he had officially claimed as his own long ago. Row after row of alphabetized horror films lined the walls, accompanied by movie posters for all the classics. Smaller shelves displayed his various horror collectibles and autographs from famous horror actors.

Joey heard his father grumbling in the back part of the basement—the laundry room. Then there was a banging sound, and his father let out a string of curse words.

"Dad?" Joey called out.

"What?" Dad said from the shadows.

"You down here?"

"You figure that out by yourself?"

Joey smiled and rolled his eyes as he followed his father's sarcastic voice to the laundry room. Dad still wore his work overalls and was crouching down beneath a network of black pipes. His hands were filthy, and he had a pile of tools spread out between his work boots.

"Whatcha doin?" Joey asked.

"Water pressure was driving me crazy, so I came down here to find the problem. And I found it." He stooped, grabbed something from his toolbox, and handed it to Joey. It was a Dracula action figure. "Wanna explain what this was doing *inside* the toilet tank?"

Joey beamed red in embarrassment. "I was playing Dracula vs. King Ape at the Eternal Springs."

"The Eternal Springs being the toilet tank?" Dad asked.

Joey nodded, ashamed. "Sorry," he said.

"Well, *Dracula* got sucked right into the valve—it was making all the pipes in the house go wacko," Dad said. "I never thought I'd say these words, but, please don't play in the toilet anymore, okay?"

"Sure," Joey said.

"Since I'm down here I figured I'd mess around with this washing machine," Dad continued. "Your mother says it doesn't work right, but between you and me, I think she's insane."

Joey laughed at Dad's claim. Like his mother, Joey's father seemed plucked straight from a 1950s sitcom, only instead of the doting father, he was more like the grouchy but loveable next-door neighbor.

"Maybe you've been having vampire doll battles inside the washing machine, too," he added, dryly.

Joey half-smiled, but he wasn't really listening. The last thing he had on his mind right now was the washing machine. He had to tell someone about the ghostly face and hand he had seen. But now, in the presence of his father, he knew how foolish he would sound.

Still, he had to try something.

"Dad…do you know anything about the house on Creep Street?" he asked cautiously.

"Creep Street?" Dad barked, looking up from his work. He furrowed his brow. "You weren't fooling around there, were you, son?"

"No, sir!" Joey said quickly. "I was just curious. Kids in town say it's haunted."

Dad laughed, coughing heavily at the end of his laughter. "That's dumb."

Joey laughed nervously. "It is dumb, isn't it? Still, it's kind of neat. I heard…the Smahs lived there?"

Dad's face suddenly looked ashen. He stood up and brushed his dirty hands on his overalls. "Where did you hear that?"

"Oh, around…"

There was a long, awkward pause. Joey could see the side of Dad's jaw clicking. The man looked deep in thought.

"Those are all just stories, Joey," Dad finally said. "It's just a house; an old, empty house. In fact, I want you to promise you'll stay out of there. Okay?"

Joey noticed that his father had become rather insistent, like something seemed to be bothering him. Not wanting to upset him, Joey quickly agreed. "Okay, I promise," he said. "Forget I said anything. I'm gonna go get ready for bed."

"Okay," Dad said and began putting away his tools.

Joey made his way back upstairs, wondering what it was about the house that had made his father so nervous.

CHAPTER FIVE

After saying goodnight to his mother, Joey flopped down on his bed and turned on the television. Max, the family's Old English Sheepdog, groggily raised his sleepy head. He stared at Joey for a moment before re-nestling comfortably against the closet door and going back to chasing cats in his sleep.

Joey stared at the television, paying half attention to the flickering picture in front of him. He was still having trouble wrapping his mind around everything he had seen that night. That old house, the ghost...it all seemed so unbelievable.

He flipped channels for a bit, but then tossed the remote aside when he saw a familiar face. Chris Lopez, host of Joey's favorite ghost-hunting show, *Spooky Mysteries,* was wandering around an abandoned farmhouse. He was a young, muscular fellow who traveled the country investigating strange and odd happenings with his camera crew. Even though Chris never seemed to find what he was looking for—namely sprits from the afterlife—Joey worshipped him.

A muffled noise sounded in the background of the house where Chris and his film crew were roaming. "Dude!" Chris yelled directly into the camera. "Did you hear that? It said my name! IT KNOWS MY NAME!"

"I think it was just a dog barking," someone off-camera said.

"SHUT UP!" Chris bellowed and ran off into the darkness.

Joey glanced at his alarm clock and saw it was just before midnight. His eyes drifted to his bookshelf. Lined up in a row, in the order of their publication, were all of the *Spook Boys* books, a series of kids' books about two adventurous brothers who were constantly getting into mischief as they explored haunted houses and spooky old castles, or tried to solve mysteries involving missing diamonds or stolen paintings. Joey envied the characters in those books—he wanted his own life to be made up of such exciting, implausible adventures. So maybe his imagination had gotten carried away this time. Maybe his mind, saturated with such fictional tales, was more than willing to play tricks on him when it came to houses like the one on Creep Street.

He shook those thoughts away. He *had* seen something, no matter what anyone said.

Restless, Joey climbed out of bed to grab a glass of water for the night, and as he walked down the hallway, he heard his parents talking to each other in hushed voices. He stopped, curious after having heard his name. He crept silently to the top of the stairs and listened.

"I think he was in that house tonight," he heard Dad say. "He was asking me all about it—he even knew the name of the family that used to live there…the Smahs."

"How on earth does he know a thing like that?" Mom demanded.

"I have no idea," Dad said.

"I bet it was Michael, your weirdo friend. "

"Don't be silly," Dad said. "Joey hardly ever sees Michael."

"He has that weird little shop over on Main Street," Mom continued, "where he sells all those weird books and other weirdo stuff. I don't even know why you're friends with him."

"Michael and I go way back!" Dad argued. "We used to throw eggs at my brother, Bart! Come to think of it, Michael was obsessed with that stupid Creep Street house when we were kids. What with all the spooky stuff that went down there."

Joey's ears pricked up.

Spooky stuff? Clearly, there is more than meets the eye about the house on Creep Street!

"Well, there you have it!" Mom said. "Joey could have easily stopped into that shop one day, and I bet that

Michael filled his head with all that morbid Creep Street stuff."

"You're crazy," Dad said. "Next thing I know, *you'll* be playing with toys in the toilet."

"What does that even mean?" Mom asked, confused.

"I'm going to bed," Dad muttered. "Good night, crazy woman."

Joey darted back into his room and shut the door as quickly and quietly as he could. He grabbed his phone and dialed Barry's number.

His friend picked up on the second ring, and sounding fully awake, said, "What's up?"

"Maybe something, I'm not sure," Joey said. "What are you doing?"

"*WrestleTime* is on," Barry responded, and over the phone, Joey could hear the roar of the crowd and the wrestlers' threats in the background. "Sorry about tonight," he then said. "You know, with the whole trick-or-treating thing."

Joey was a little surprised by his friend's sudden apology, and he was also surprised that he had actually almost forgotten about the trick-or-treating thing, so consumed he was with the house on Creep Street. "Yeah, well..."

"Kevin was the one who brought it up in the first place—"

"Big surprise."

"—but he does make a good point. We're gonna be teenagers soon. Maybe it's time we gave it up."

"Listen, that's a whole other issue," Joey said. "There is something weird about that house we were in tonight. I know you guys don't believe me—"

"It is a little unbelievable," Barry agreed.

"I know," Joey admitted. "I *swear* to you, though, I saw something."

Barry didn't say anything, and for a moment, background noise from the wrestling match filled the empty silence.

"I just think we should try to find out more about the place," Joey continued.

"*We*?" Barry clarified.

"Yeah, man," Joey said. "I know neither of you believe in this stuff, but I need you guys to back me up! Besides, what else are we doing?"

"When do you wanna start?" Barry sighed, seeing Joey was not going to let this go so easily.

Joey couldn't help but smile. "How about tomorrow?"

A large crashing sound in the background—followed by a whoop-whoop from Barry—was his response. "Oh man, Jammers Slammin' just totally power-smashed Money Man onto his skull!"

Joey laughed. He was glad he had called his friend. "See you tomorrow."

He hung up the phone and clicked off his light. He stared at the dark ceiling and wondered what he was getting himself into. Before drifting off to sleep, he had a feeling that once he began digging into the past, he might learn more about the house on Creep Street than he ever wanted to know.

* * *

Barry hung up with his friend and turned back to the television. As Jammers Slammin' bounced a fake chair off Money Man's back, Barry tried to contain his excitement, or he risked waking up his whole house. He watched the wrestlers pummel each other and couldn't help but feel in awe of them. He knew all of it was fake—knew that these wrestlers were really just actors playing a part, and that all of their "fighting" had been carefully choreographed to look realistic while remaining safe—but he was still fascinated by it all. The wrestlers were strong and popular and seemed to get all the girls, and that was something Barry wanted more than anything. But it was his weight that held him back, made him doubt himself.

He once tried to explain to his friends that it was a medical condition that made him so big—something having to do with his thyroid, which affected the way his body absorbed the food he ate. But his friends would laugh and say, "Sure, Barry. Whatever you say. Would you like to eat an entire ham?"

That's not to say Barry didn't enjoy his fair share of junk food. He was, after all, a twelve-year-old boy. But still: jokes like the ones his friends made hurt his feelings. He knew them well enough to know they didn't mean their jokes to be malicious—that they were just having a laugh—but that didn't mean they hurt any less. He often considered telling them straight away that their jokes upset him, but because he didn't have many other friends besides Joey and Kevin, he didn't want to risk pushing them away forever. So he let them crack their jokes and he pretended they didn't bother him. A small price to pay, he reasoned.

On the television screen, Jammers Slammin' shot a cannon ball into Money Man's stomach and the audience went wild.

Barry hooted once before clamping his hands over his mouth.

THREE DAYS TILL HALLOWEEN

CHAPTER SIX

It was Saturday morning as Joey rode his bike down the street to Barry's house—a very short trip.

It was a beautiful autumn morning—the type of autumn morning that some people think exists only in paintings and dreams. The air was crisp and cool, and the leaves were every shade of red and orange.

But Joey didn't let himself get lost in the time of year he loved so much. No, there was more to learn about the Smah house. Because of how otherworldly the events from the previous night had seemed, Joey wanted—no, *needed* – to find out the story behind the place. There was *something* going on in that house.

He skidded to a stop in front of Barry's house. On the overgrown lawn of the quaint ranch home stood Sandra, Barry's older (and very pretty) sister. She was raking leaves and looked somewhat bored with the task. Joey's heart fluttered as he saw her in a red down vest and skinny jeans. She looked up at him, a strand of black hair blowing from her face. The world seemed to come alive with white light as she slowly blinked her deep brown eyes and parted her full lips.

"What do you want, dork?" she growled.

"Uh, is Barry here?" Joey asked, his voice squeaking.

"Where else would he be? Besides the pie store?" Sandra muttered, rolling her eyes and going back to raking.

Barry came bounding out of the garage with his pink bike. It had belonged to Sandra when she was his age, and his parents had neglected to buy him a bike of his own.

"Hi, Joey!" Barry said cheerfully. The bike was a little big for him, and he had trouble mounting it.

"Where are you two dopes going?" Sandra asked.

"Just out!" Barry said, smiling. "Tell Mom I'll be back later!"

"I'll get right on that, master," Sandra said sarcastically.

"Uh, bye, Sandra..." Joey croaked.

She did not respond.

The boys pedaled down King Street toward Main.

"So, what's the plan?" Barry asked, trying to eat a candy bar without losing control of his bike.

"We gotta convince Kevin to get on board," Joey said. "Even if I am still a little mad at him for bailing on trick-or-treating this year."

The boys were soon in the middle of town and riding down Main Street, which was made up of small shops and restaurants. They passed Town Hall, and then Resurrection Cemetery, which was located right behind it.

Soon the friends were on the other side of town, entering Stine Court, where Kevin's family lived in their rather large house. Kevin was in the driveway dribbling a basketball.

"Yo, dudes," he said, sinking the ball into the regulation-size basket at the end of the driveway.

"Kevin, you have to come with us," Joey said.

"Where?"

"The library," Joey said.

"Oh, how exciting," Kevin said sarcastically.

"Man, you didn't say anything about the library!" cried Barry, who had assessed overdue fines for several science books he had borrowed the previous year and then lost somewhere in the labyrinth of his room. He hadn't set foot inside the library since, for fear of being promptly arrested by the library police and serving time in library jail, where he imagined the bars were made out of the spines of old hardback books.

"It'll be fine, they won't know," Joey told his friend.

"Why are you going to the library?" Kevin asked. "On a *weekend,* no less? Sounds pretty lame."

"It's important," Joey answered. "I have to find out about something."

"About what?" Kevin asked.

"The house on Creep Street," Joey said.

"Oh man, not this again," Kevin started, already losing interest in the conversation. "Joey, it's just a creepy old house."

"Kevin, I saw something in there last night!" Joey insisted. "I know you don't believe me. And that's fine. You don't have to. But all I'm asking is that you give this a chance."

"Why?" Kevin asked, sinking another basket.

Joey thought long and hard. "Because…because maybe there's more to this little town than meets the eye; because maybe there's something beyond the little stores, and the picket fences, and the friendly neighbors. Maybe there's a dark side that hasn't ever been explored before—and we can be the first to explore it. Maybe there really are things that go bump in the night. Maybe we can find them…together."

A hush fell upon the boys. The breeze picked up and scattered more dead leaves across the street.

"But why?" Kevin asked.

"Just shut up and get your bike," Joey said angrily.

"Fine," Kevin said.

* * *

Inside the library, the boys crowded around a microfilm machine. It had taken at least twenty minutes before they figured out how to work the ancient relic, and now Joey was carefully spinning the knob, afraid to miss a potential discovery. They scanned through old issues of the town newspaper, *The Blackwood Blackboard*, searching for information. And they were coming up empty.

"It would help if we knew what year that house was built," Joey whispered, frustrated. "I don't even know where to start looking."

"Type in 'spooky house'!" Barry suggested.

"This isn't a computer, Barry," Kevin said.

"Oh."

"Joey, this is hopeless," Kevin sighed. "Let's just throw stuff off the overpass."

"Wait, there!" Joey said, stopping the machine. On the yellow, washed-out screen was an issue of *The Blackwood Blackboard* dated November 1st, 1945.

The headline read, in bold black letters:

HALLOWEEN MURDER ON CREEP STREET

"Murder!" all three boys said loudly.

Before they could begin to read the article, they sensed someone step up behind them.

"Ahem!" said a stern voice.

The boys turned and saw Mrs. Chins, the head librarian. She loomed over them, her blue-tinted hair styled in a bun on her egg-shaped head. "You three boys are being awfully loud!"

"Oh, sorry," Joey said, embarrassed.

"Wait…" Mrs. Chins said, her eyes narrowing behind her large glasses. "You there—aren't you the boy with the late fees on all the science books?"

"Cheese it!" Barry yelled and darted from his chair, running to the library exit. Kevin and Joey looked at each other and then ran after him.

An irate Mrs. Chins glared at them as they fled out the door.

* * *

"We were so close to finding out what happened in that house!" Joey shouted as the boys rode their bikes up Main Street.

"Sorry," Barry said ashamedly. "Told you it was a bad idea to go there."

Joey's mind was reeling now. It had been there in black and white: **HALLOWEEN MURDER ON CREEP STREET.**

"I knew something was up!" he proudly said as they rode down the street. "Murder!"

"Oh, come on, Joey," Kevin said. "Just because there was a murder on Creep Street doesn't mean it was at *that* house. It could've happened at one of the other houses before they were torn down."

But Joey knew in his gut the murder had taken place in the Smah house—he didn't have to be one of the "Spook Boys" to solve *that* mystery. He didn't know *how* he knew, but he did. And the sight of the ghostly face in the upstairs window—or the beckoning finger and menacing voice—wasn't exactly making him doubt his instincts.

I know I'm right about this, Joey thought. *And I can't wait to rub it in their faces when I find proof.*

A light bulb then went off in Joey's head and he grinned at his newest scheme.

"I'll make you a bet, Kevin," he began. "If it turns out the murder *did* take place in that house, then you *have* to go trick-or-treating on Halloween. We *all* do!"

Kevin rolled his eyes and looked at Barry for support.

"Oh, come on, Kevin," Barry said. "Trick-or-treating isn't so bad. Free candy!"

"Fine," Kevin sighed. "*If* it turns out the house on Creep Street was the scene of a murder, then maybe—*maybe*—I'll consider trick-or-treating."

The three boys spit in their palms and high-fived to seal the deal.

Joey felt pretty good—they were one step closer to finding out what had occurred on Creep Street, and now it looked like Halloween might be salvaged after all.

"Now what?" Kevin asked, turning his lucky hat around backwards.

But Joey didn't know what to do next. He didn't even know what to think. Then the newspaper headlines of Halloween murder flashed through his mind again.

Joey's eyes lit up.

"We're going to the cemetery!"

"The cemetery?" Kevin and Barry asked in unison.

"Why?" Kevin added.

"To find the graves of the Smahs!"

CHAPTER SEVEN

"The boneyard? Are you nutso?" Barry asked, breathing heavily from the boys' furious pedaling to Resurrection Cemetery.

"It will prove once and for all that the murder took place in *that* house," Joey argued. "That newspaper said *someone* was murdered on Creep Street on Halloween, 1945, right? So, we check to see if a Smah is buried in the cemetery, and if so, we check the date of death."

"Joey, you should consider doing something a bit less depressing with your life," said Kevin. "Give all this murder and blood stuff a rest, and maybe perfect a great three-point shot!" He took his hands off his handlebars to mimic shooting a basketball and nearly lost control of the bike.

"Who has time for basketball when we've got haunted houses?" Joey scoffed, and then skidded just outside the thick bronze gate of the cemetery.

"Is it open?" Barry asked, peering through the bars.

"Of course it's open," said Kevin. "Cemeteries are *always* open."

"Wrong, boyo," a gruff voice suddenly boomed. An ancient man had appeared on the other side of the gates, eyeing all three boys suspiciously. The boys couldn't help but take a cautious step back. Barry whimpered and nearly toppled off his too-large girl's bike.

"I close it all up every night at sundown, and open every morning at sunrise," the ancient man continued. "This ain't no night club. It's a place of rest. "

"Who are you?" Joey finally managed, stepping closer.

The old man stooped to look from one boy's face to the next. "I'm the caretaker. I'm in charge of keeping up the place, and keeping trouble out of it." He glared at the boys. "Are you trouble?"

"No sir," Joey said. "Can we come in?"

The old caretaker grabbed one of the bars, as if preventing Joey from pushing it open. "What business do a bunch of bike-kids have in a cemetery?"

"We're just here to find a grave," said Barry. The obviousness of this answer would surely have resulted in some kind of sarcastic comments from his friends had they not been currently terrified.

"Well, I should hope so," the caretaker grumbled. "Cuz if you're lookin' for arcade games or candy machines, you're in the wrong place."

It was impossible for the boys to determine the caretaker's age, but their guesses would have been somewhere around 107. He was very tall and gaunt, dressed in filthy jeans, a red plaid shirt, and a badly worn denim jacket. His head was full of stark white hair that drooped down into a thick, unmanaged beard, which probably housed any number of insects and small rodents. His face was withered, filled with decades of wrinkles.

"Can you tell us if anyone with the last name of Smah is buried here?" Joey asked through the gates.

The caretaker stared at Joey for a long time, his eyes growing even narrower. Something else registered on the old caretaker's face. Unless it was Joey's imagination, it had seemed to be…alarm. Or fear.

"Why do you want to know that?" the caretaker demanded.

"We're trying to find out about the hou—" Barry began before Kevin cut him off.

"It's for a school project."

"Nonsense," said the caretaker. "No school makes kids romp around graveyards. Not even crazy schools!"

The boys exchanged subtle confused glances.

"One time we *did* have to come here for a school assignment," said Barry, betraying Kevin's lie. "And I dropped my keys and never found them, and I was really worried that zombies would unlock my front door and eat my knees!"

"Thanks for that bit of information," Kevin said to Barry through gritted teeth.

"Sir, please, we're not here to do any harm," Joey assured the old caretaker. "We just want to find the Smah grave."

The caretaker shook his head. "Folks oughta leave certain things alone!"

The boys stared at him, waiting, and the old caretaker could see they had no intention of leaving.

"Sir…this is a public place, after all," Kevin said to the old caretaker, without fear. "We have a right to be here."

Joey resisted the urge to look at his friend in wide-eyed shock and puke his heart out.

The old caretaker's shoulders sank, and his lips slightly parted to reveal scarce and yellow teeth. "Don't make me regret telling ya, hear?"

The boys nodded.

"Older graves are right smack in the middle of the place. You'll find Smah there, in the thirteenth row. And you be careful with those tombstones, because they're older than me. They'll crumble right in your hands if you mess around with 'em."

"Yes, sir," Joey said. The old man stepped back and pulled open the gate, which squealed with age, allowing Joey to ease inside on his bike. Kevin and Barry slinked in just behind him. They softly pedaled their bikes in the direction the caretaker had specified.

"Thirteenth row," Kevin dryly said once they were out of earshot. "Perfect."

The deeper the boys pedaled into Resurrection Cemetery, the thicker the trees grew, and the darker their surroundings became. Though it was still early in what had been a very bright day, their environment had suddenly become uninviting and ominous. Unseen birds cawed at them, and tree branches creaked and cracked.

"This is the pits," Barry said. "I could be home watching *WrestleTime* reruns."

"But you'd be missing out on tripping through a graveyard, dude!" Kevin said and shot Joey a sarcastic grin.

"You know, Kevin, sometimes—"

"Look!" Barry suddenly shouted, and the boys' bikes skidded to a halt.

"Wow!" Joey said, eyeing the mammoth tombstone that stood larger than all three of the boys. The name SMAH was engraved across its wide face, and in front of that structure were three smaller stones with rounded edges and tinged in light gray.

The boys tentatively slid off their bikes and let them drop to the ground as they stared in awe at the forged flint-gray rock before them.

"Guys, look!" Joey shouted. "They're all here! The whole Smah family!"

Most of the engravings had worn over time, but the words were mostly legible:

BENNINGTON SMAH
May 15, 1909 – December 16, 1944
Husband - Father - Fallen Soldier

"Whoa, he was a soldier?" Kevin asked. "And 1944…that'd be World War II, right?"

"I think so," Barry said.

Joey was barely listening, as he was busy checking the next small tombstone and tracing his finger across the name.

BETTY SMAH
February 3, 1911 – December 25, 1972
Wife & Mother

"Wow, she died on Christmas," Barry said. "That's sad."

"People don't die on Christmas," Kevin said. "They off themselves." He drew his finger across his throat and made the appropriate noise with his mouth. Barry chuckled and pushed him.

Joey nearly lunged to the next stone. He crouched to read the final name.

ROBERT SMAH
April 13, 1933 – October 31, 1945
Son

"It's him!" Joey declared. "Bob Smah!"

Kevin and Barry ducked down to read the tombstone.

"That newspaper article was from the next day!" Joey cried. "Bob Smah was the one who was murdered on Creep Street! On Halloween!"

"Wow, he was our age," Kevin said. "Who would murder a kid?"

"A psycho," Barry answered. "Guys, this is sick. I don't feel right messing around with this."

"We're not messing around," Joey argued. "This is just another piece of the puzzle. We proved there was a murder, and that it took place in that house. And *now* we know who was killed."

"Right," said Kevin. "But…now what?"

"We find out exactly what happened," Joey said. "It *has* to be Bob Smah's ghost I saw that night. When a person dies a violent death, their spirit stays behind. I read that in one of Chris Lopez's ghost books."

"*Ghost* books?" both Kevin and Barry asked through laughter. Joey ignored them, looking down again at Bob Smah's tombstone.

"Okay, so how do we find out what happened?" Barry asked. "We can't go back to that library, dudes! We just can't! I'll be paying off those fines until I'm wearing old man clothes!"

"I'll bet that caretaker knows what happened," Kevin offered.

Joey grinned at him, pleasantly surprised his friend was finally participating. "Glad to hear you're on the team, Kev."

"Friends forever," he said in response and the boys bumped fists.

"Two dorks," said Barry.

"You boys find what you were lookin' for?" asked a voice. They gasped and turned quickly to see the old caretaker again.

"Don't DO that!" Barry said, grabbing his chest to calm his racing heart.

The caretaker grunted and looked past the boys to the tall tombstone. Sadness loomed over his face and Joey sensed it immediately.

"Do you know what happened that night?" Joey asked. "The night Bob Smah was murdered?

The sadness remained, and it looked to Joey that the caretaker might talk, but just as quickly as the sadness had come, it was soon replaced with darkness and anger.

"What makes you think it was murder that done 'im in?" he demanded.

Joey's heart started to race. He suddenly realized that being in this cemetery with this furious old creep was the last place he wanted to be.

"But…the newspaper *said* it was murder," Joey managed in a small voice. "Are you saying the papers were wrong?"

"I'm sayin' not everything is what it seems," the caretaker said, his voice barely containing his fury. "And I'm sayin' to let 'im rest in peace! That kid had a tough life before he died! He was picked on and bullied; hadn't a friend in the world! He don't need you jumpin' on his grave, dredgin' up all his misery like a bunch of cheap dime-store detectives!"

Joey's mind was working overtime, trying to figure out what it was he had said to set off the caretaker. "Sir, we're only trying—"

"Get out!" the caretaker bellowed.

Barry shrieked in unmitigated fear.

"Get out!" the caretaker growled again. "And keep your noses out of this Smah business, ya hear? Ain't no good will come of it!"

The boys jumped on their bikes and pedaled quickly down the bumpy path and breezed out the front entrance as the caretaker continued to shout at them from within the bowels of the cemetery.

"What a psycho!" Kevin cried.

"That guy nearly gave me a heart attack!" Barry shouted.

But Joey was undaunted by the old caretaker's explosion of anger. He was more frustrated that the real story of the house on Creep Street continued to evade him.

"If that old caretaker didn't want to spill the beans, then fine," Joey said. "But *somebody* in this town has to know what really happened."

Like a sign from above, at that exact moment, the boys found themselves riding right by a store called *Michael's Cabinet of Curiosities*. Joey suddenly remembered overhearing his parents' whispered argument about his father's friend, Michael—about his weird shop, and his knowledge of Creep Street.

"There's our next stop!" Joey answered, pointing to the door. "The guy who owns this store is a friend of my father! I'll bet he knows a thing or two about what happened!"

As the boys climbed off their bikes, Joey noticed that the previously bright day had slowly begun rolling over with dark gray storm clouds. Other people in the street even looked up at the ominous skies with alarm on their faces, as if a storm had been the last thing they expected on such a sunny day.

Joey couldn't help but notice how much the storm seemed to mirror exactly what he felt about his own hometown of Blackwood. On the surface, it was such a nice and cheerful place—even old fashioned—but like storm clouds, Creep Street sat in almost constant shadow.

A dark stain in an otherwise perfect place to live...

CHAPTER EIGHT

By the time the boys entered Michael's store, the sky above was mostly dark. A loud bell above the door clanged and the boys were hit with the unmistakable smell of old books.

The store itself seemed endless, stretching into a dark oblivion. There was no rhyme or reason to how it was arranged. Old wooden shelves were set up in zigzag patterns and crammed with books, mason jars full of mysterious liquid, metallic statues, hand-carved wooden ducks, goblets, and many other oddities.

"Check this out!" Barry said, picking up a taxidermy rat mounted on a wooden board. "It looks like Kevin's mom!"

"Put that down!" Joey said. "Don't break anything. I don't want to get Michael upset."

"Speaking of Michael, where is he?" Kevin asked.

Joey looked around, realizing Kevin had made a good point. Other than the boys, the store seemed empty. There was a small counter to the right, and behind it was a large shelf full of books, with titles like *Witchcraft and You;*

How to Summon and Expel Demons; The Real Dracula; and *Harriet Goes to Lunch (With a Ghost).*

"Hello?" Joey called out. The boys stepped further into the jumbled store, approaching the counter. There was a small hand-bell with a sign reading *Please Ring for Service.*

Joey tapped the bell and they waited. Barry tapped the bell several times in a row until Joey grabbed his hand. "Please stop."

"Where the heck is this guy?" Kevin asked.

Joey bent over the counter and gasped. Lying on the floor behind the counter—facedown—was Michael.

Barry looked over the counter to see for himself. "Oh my gosh!" he said. "He's dead! Let's run home!"

Suddenly, Michael sprang up from the floor. "Ahhh!" he began exclaiming, causing the boys to also cry out in shock—the four of them now yelling "Ahhh!" almost in harmony.

Barry stumbled backward and knocked over several stacks of books.

Michael then adjusted his glasses and looked at them, beaming a smile. "Customers!" he happily called.

"Are you okay?" Joey cried, utterly mystified.

"Why were you lying on the floor?" Kevin asked, catching his breath.

"The rug had a strange smell," Michael said, wrinkling his nose. "I was trying to determine its origin."

Joey and Kevin were speechless. Barry threw his hands up and looked around the store and muttered, "Seriously, what is this?"

Michael was well over six feet tall and balding, the remainder of his hair in graying tufts around his ears. He wore a faded brown suit with a skinny black tie, complete with a silver tie bar. The yellow store light glinted off his coke-bottle glasses.

"Welcome!" he cried, stretching out his hands. "Welcome to *Michael's Cabinet of Curiosities!* I'm your host, Michael!"

"Hi, Michael," Barry said nervously.

"So, what can I do for three boys such as yourselves? Can I offer you a plastic pumpkin?"

Michael reached beneath the counter and came up with a plastic jack-o-lantern.

"Very popular this time of year! Or how about this?"

He threw the pumpkin aside and pulled out a Whoopee cushion.

"Make all your friends laugh their brains out! Or there's this!"

He tossed the Whoopee cushion aside, reached under the counter once more, and pulled out a living snake. It slithered up his arm and flicked its tongue at the boys.

Kevin screamed in fear and hid behind Barry.

"Michael, do you recognize me?" Joey asked, cautiously eyeing the snake. "I'm Joey Tonelli. You're friends with my father?"

"Ah, yes!" Michael said. "You're the younger one! The one always playing with toilet dolls!"

"Right," Joey said quickly, turning bright red.

"What brings you to my shop?"

"We're here for information..." Barry said, unsurely.

Michael's eyes lit up. "Information?"

"Yes, sir," Joey said.

"Well then, you've come to the right place!" Michael said, overjoyed. "I am a man who has plenty of information! For instance, did you know cow babies are born with two heads, and one of those heads falls off before its sixth birthday?"

"That's true," Kevin sarcastically agreed, nodding to his friends.

"We want information about the Smah house," Joey said, lowering his voice to a whisper. "The house on Creep Street."

The light went out of Michael's eyes, but a sly smile stretched over his round face. He let the snake down, which slithered away behind some boxes, and pointed at Joey. "You're a boy not interested in the norm; a boy who isn't content with the sunny side of things; a boy who craves the shadows, and who flings open the closet door in hopes of finding monsters. Ah, yes...I know your kind well, Joey Tonelli."

Joey gulped. He felt the hairs on the back of his neck standing up.

"So, it's information on the Smah house you seek?" Michael asked. "Well then, follow me!" He turned and retreated into the dimly lit back of the store.

The boys looked at each other.

"Let's leave!" Kevin whispered. "He's crazy!"

"I think he's fun!" Barry said.

"Fun?" Kevin argued. "Did you *not* hear that baby cow head thing?"

"We can't chicken out now, dudes," Joey said. "C'mon!"

They followed Michael through the store to a small personal office. Candles flickered on a desk. Old paintings lined the walls, along with blurry photographs from times long forgotten. A ratty couch sat in a corner. He pulled out a large leather chair from his desk and spun it around. The boys gasped when they saw a large black raven sitting in the chair. It spread its wings and squawked at them.

"What the—Nutty! I told you to stay out of my office!" Michael said. He swatted at the raven, which flew into the air, squawked once more, and flapped its wings out of the office.

"If this gets any more eccentric, my head is gonna fall off," Kevin whispered to Joey.

Michael sat down at his desk and opened a drawer. He pulled out a large photo album and flipped it open, turning the pages at a rapid pace until he found what he was looking for: a photo—the same photo Joey had seen in the Creep Street house! The Smahs grinned in their family portrait, blissfully unaware of the terrible fate that awaited them in their futures.

"The Smah name goes far back in Blackwood history," Michael said. "There were Smahs living here as early as 1804, when the town was founded. This here album belonged to the newest—and last—generation of the Smah family."

"Wow!" Barry said.

Michael spun the album and slid it to Joey, who flipped through its pages. Pictures of Bennington, Betty, and Bob Smah littered every page. Their smiles were wide and their happiness nearly palpable. However, after a while, Joey noticed that Bob's father stopped appearing; the photos were only of Bob and his mom, and the look of subtle sadness in their eyes was unmistakable. Joey also noticed that in all of these later photos, Bob was wearing something pinned to his shirt: a medal of some kind—too small in the photos to really decipher.

"There are no more living Smahs," Michael continued. "The last of the Smah line was this boy, Bob." He tapped the face of the boy in the photo. "And, well, he didn't live long enough to have children of his own."

The three boys suddenly had the shivers.

"Yes, we found out about his murder! What happened?" Joey asked, his gaze fixed on Bob.

"Ah, yes," Michael said slyly. "His...*murder*." He looked at Joey and cast him a peculiar smile—one that suggested he was privy to a little-known secret.

"Do you mean it *wasn't* murder?" Joey asked.

"I never said that," Michael said, holding up his hands. "It's just that no one really knows *what* happened to young Bob Smah that Halloween night. It's a mystery—perhaps the biggest mystery Blackwood's ever had."

First murder, and now an unsolved mystery? Joey thought. *No wonder Dad was so unnerved about this house!*

Michael rose from his chair and flung open a nearby closet. He dug through it, muttering to himself, and then pulled out a metal film canister.

"What's that?" Kevin asked.

"The Smah family's home movies!" Michael said proudly.

"Why do *you* have all this Smah stuff?" Kevin asked.

"Because I'm a collector," Michael grinned. "I collect everything in this town. Sooner or later, it all ends up in my store." From the closet, he retrieved an old film projector and loaded up the film. "Have a seat, boys!" he said.

As the friends sat down on Michael's ratty couch, Joey noticed Barry had a bowl of popcorn.

"Where'd you get that?"

"Found it," Barry said, shrugging.

"Only Big Barry could find popcorn in an antique store!" Kevin laughed. Barry glanced down into the bowl, but said nothing.

Michael killed the lights and fired up the projector. Moving images were cast against the bare wall opposite the couch.

The footage was old and grainy: colorless, soundless, and moving at an unnaturally fast speed. The boys watched, transfixed, as Betty Smah stood in her garden, watering plants. She suddenly looked up, noticed she was being filmed, and threw her head back in a silent laugh. She was beautiful, her hair styled, her eyes large and clear. The footage cut abruptly to Bennington Smah in a pair of dirty jeans as he hammered on some raw, unfinished wood. He saluted the camera and waved, then smiled. The footage cut again. There was young Bob, doing cartwheels in the backyard. The house on Creep Street stood behind him, and it looked completely different. It was not falling apart or boarded up. The house was full of life…unlike now, where its only occupant was the dead.

"The Smahs were quite popular in the community," Michael said, as he continued to rattle off what information he had on the family. "They were well-liked and described as kind and loving people."

The footage was now of Bob and Bennington on the front lawn throwing a baseball back and forth. Bob caught the ball proudly in his mitt, and held it up for the camera to see.

Joey suddenly felt very sad watching the footage. The people in it had been alive at one time, and their futures were only bright. Their world was full of endless possibilities.

And then something had changed.

"They were a typical American family," Michael said from the darkness. "In 1944, shortly after D-Day, Bennington Smah decided to enlist in the army, and so he went off to war. He was killed a few months later during the Battle of the Bulge after having saved his whole platoon from a grenade. He was awarded the Medal of Honor posthumously."

"What's *posthumously*?" Barry whispered.

"Dead," Joey said sadly.

"Betty and Bob were devastated by this, of course," Michael continued. "But they carried on...at first."

More footage showed Bob on Christmas morning sitting in front of the tree. The boy was excited over his many gifts, but his eyes still reflected the loss of his father.

Another image, presumably filmed by Bob due to its shaky nature and low height, showed his mother sitting by a window and looking at something out there in the past. She looked much different than she had at the beginning of the footage. Now she looked like a woman completely lost; her clothes wrinkled, her hair a mess, her eyes deep and hollow.

"The loss of Bob's father was too much for Betty," Michael said. "She started to 'crack up,' to use a blunt term. Started wandering the streets of Blackwood late at night. One day the police had to be called because she had stumbled into Blackwood General, barefoot and still in her nightgown, and started taking jars of preserves off the shelf and smashing them. She got in more trouble with the law once she started breaking into people's houses at night."

"To rob them?" Joey asked, enthralled and a little creeped-out by this whole story.

"No, no," Michael said. "Nothing like that. She would just enter people's homes and the owners would find her sleeping on their couch, or sitting at their kitchen tables mumbling incoherently. Like she were desperate to live any life that wasn't her own."

In the footage, Betty suddenly noticed Bob was filming her. She looked furious, shouting silently, pressing her hand over the camera lens and engulfing the room in darkness for a brief moment.

The footage then switched to Bob at the beach, kneeling at the shoreline and building a sand castle.

"The whole town started to gossip about Betty," Michael continued. "Her actions turned her and Bob into outsiders. The boys at school teased him mercilessly over it. Betty knew things had to change. She started to see a doctor—in private, of course. Back then, any sort of mental health treatment was looked upon as scandalous. But with the doctor's help, she began to get better. Things began to improve for the Smah family."

On the beach, Bob Smah stood up and pointed at something off-camera. The person filming, likely Betty, turned around and focused on the sky. Dark, stormy clouds were starting to roll in against the previously sunny day.

Just like the sky above the boys at that very moment…

"And then, on Halloween night, 1945, more tragedy befell the Smahs," said Michael. "It had been a very popular Halloween, and they had run out of candy. Betty had left the house to go down to the corner store to buy some more. She was only gone for five minutes—or so she claimed. But when she came back, she found her son…"

The camera zoomed in on Bob's grinning face.

"…dead. In the basement. Perhaps murdered, like the newspapers say."

"By who?" Kevin asked.

"No one knows," Michael answered. "The presumed killer was never caught. Not long after, it's believed that Betty Smah went completely mad. She had already been on the brink, of course, and this just pushed her over the edge. Following Bob's funeral, she claimed their house became haunted. She said the plumbing never worked right afterwards, and that she heard strange noises at night. Of course, everyone thought her grief had finally gotten the better of her. She became a total recluse, never leaving the house. She passed away many years later—some believe by her own hand. No one has lived in the house since. It has a bad reputation, you see. No one wants to dwell there now."

No one except ghosts, Joey thought.

"Cool story," Kevin said. "I guess."

"It's *not* cool, Kevin," Joey barked. "It's terrible."

Kevin was silent, feeling slightly embarrassed by his apathy.

The film ran out on the reel, sputtering. Michael turned on the lights.

"Is the house haunted?" Joey asked.

Michael smiled. "I don't know…is it?"

"Has anyone ever seen a ghost there?"

"Oh, some people have *claimed* to," Michael said, sitting down in his chair. "But most folks don't believe those claims."

"I believe them," Joey whispered.

"And why is that?"

Joey got to his feet. "Because I've seen one, too."

Michael looked at Joey, a surprised look on his face. But then he smiled, ever so slightly.

"Thanks, Michael," Joey said quickly and ran from the room without looking back. Kevin and Barry ran after him.

The storm that had earlier teased its presence was now in full force. The wind had picked up and thunder rumbled. Though it was still early in the day, the ferocious storm clouds darkened the sky, and it appeared as if nighttime had arrived early.

"Joey, what's wrong?" Barry asked when they caught up with him outside.

"It's *all* wrong," Joey said, shaking his head. "Bob Smah was just a kid! He was just like us, but he died for no reason! And after everything that happened, his mom couldn't take it and went crazy! Nothing that happened to that family was fair!"

A moment of realization stopped his rant and he calmed himself. "No wonder his ghost is still in that house. He must be so...angry."

"Joey, c'mon," Kevin said. "Who do you think you are? Your hero, Chris Lopez? You need to drop this ghost stuff."

"No!" Joey said, and thunder boomed. "We've gotta do something!"

"What?" Barry asked.

"We've gotta help Bob Smah rest in peace!" Joey shouted over the wind.

Lightning tore across the dark sky.

* * *

Michael watched through his storefront window as the boys huddled outside on the sidewalk. He soon turned and made his way back through his store and to his office, where he began removing the filmstrip reel from his projector.

The Smahs... he thought to himself. *I haven't thought about them in years…*

After placing the film reel back into its canister, his eyes were drawn to the open album sitting on his desk. He stepped closer and peered down at the photo of young Bob Smah standing in front of his house.

The house on Creep Street.

The phrase someone from town would use when they wanted to invoke a feeling of unease when trying to scare another person. As an adult, Michael was now able to separate fact from fiction, as well as pretend drama from reality. What is lore today was nothing but pain and misery for the Smah family all those years ago. Bob had died several years before Michael was born, and as a child, the tragedy of what occurred was overtaken and camouflaged by its new label as simple Blackwood legend. Much like Joey, young Michael had been intensely interested in that house—and in "crazy old Betty Smah." He sighed, remembering how, in their youth, he and Joey's father had snuck over to the house to get a glimpse at what she was up to, or what she looked like.

With a husband killed in a war and a son likely murdered, she was the town black sheep. She made kids curious and adults leery. Michael remembered, upon looking through her scummy, unclean windows, how frail and tortured she was, how beaten down her life had made her. At that moment, even as a young boy, he remembered feeling incredibly sorry for her. And he remembered that what most townspeople considered Blackwood trivia was actually a lived lifetime of pain and despair of a ruined life. It was because of this that his eyes suddenly opened as a child and he saw how Betty Smah was treated by members of the town. The awful things people said about her. The terrible things they implied about her son's death. She had been bullied and tormented—not with hurtful comments, or vandalism, but with distrustful eyes, and hushed whispers as she came around a corner. It had been his first lesson in how awful people could be to each other—especially to those who were different, or strange, or weak. And he saw what resulted from such maltreatment.

He sighed once more and slowly closed the Smah family album. He picked it up, held it for a moment, and then placed it back into one of his many drawers. He sat down at his desk and stared at the wall.

Some people are doomed before they're even born.

* * *

The boys grabbed their bikes outside Michael's store, eager to escape the morbid past that he had resurrected for them. They each hopped on and took off down the street, the wind of the oncoming storm at their backs. As they rode, a realization popped into Kevin's head.

"So, I guess I have to go trick-or-treating after all, huh?" Kevin shouted into the wind to his friend.

"What? Why?" Joey asked, his gaze fixed on the stormy October sky.

"The murder. Our bet. You won!"

"I guess I did," Joey said absently. He had been so swept up in the tragedy of the Smahs that the Halloween bet had slipped his mind, and seemed almost silly now.

"Catch you dorks later!" Kevin said, shaking his head, but smiling. He pedaled away toward his house.

"So...you know what happened now," Barry said, through his huffing and puffing. "To Bob, I mean. He died in that house. We know it was him now."

"Yeah," Joey said, softly. But he didn't feel satisfied, or relieved, or anything he thought he would feel after hearing the real story. A boy was still dead, after having lived a miserable life. And he may very well be haunting his old childhood home, trapped, with no way to escape.

No, Joey didn't feel satisfied at all.

After Joey and Barry parted ways, Joey pulled his bike into his driveway, eager to get out of the rain that was sure to come.

Dad was unhooking his boat from the hitch on his van, and Joey remembered hearing his father mention that he'd had plans that morning to go fishing with Joey's Uncle Bart.

"Hi, Dad," Joey said, dropping his bike on the lawn. "How was fishing?"

"Caught some fish," Dad said, looking intently at a piece of paper.

"Did Uncle Bart go with you?"

"He sure did. We had a time or two," he answered, though his voice suggested he couldn't have meant it any less.

Joey laughed slightly and went into the house.

* * *

At the dinner table later, Mario threw a dinner roll right at Joey's head while their parents weren't looking.

"What the he—" Joey yelled.

"No bad language at the dinner table, Joey," Mom said, cutting Joey off mid-cuss as she served the pasta and broccoli.

"How many fish did you catch today, Pop?" Mario asked, taking a huge bite out of a breadstick and chewing it with his mouth open.

"Enough to fit in my bucket," Dad said and began to eat.

"So, Joey, what will be your costume for Halloweens?" Mom asked. She always called it *Halloweens.* No one ever asked why. It was just one of her many quirks.

"I dunno," Joey said, pushing the food around on his plate. "I might not go out this year."

"Oh, but you love Halloweens," Mom said.

"I know. It's just…I had to force Kevin and Barry into it. They don't even want to go."

"Why on earth not?" Mom asked, sounding concerned. "Did you boys have a fight?"

"No. I guess they think we're too old now."

"You *are* too old," Dad said and belched. "When I was your age, I wasn't tricking around. I had a job at the lumberyard, working from six in the morning till nine at night. And one day, Smitty the foreman, cut his entire elbow off—"

"Don't listen to your father, dear," Mom said. "You're never too old to have fun."

Joey smiled, feeling slightly comforted. But the Smah house invaded his thoughts. It loomed in his mind the way it loomed on the dark, deserted street it occupied.

He had a sudden flash of that boney white hand and shivered.

TWO DAYS TILL HALLOWEEN

CHAPTER NINE

The next morning, Joey sat glumly in front of the television in his bedroom, watching an episode of *Spooky Mysteries*. Host Chris Lopez was running around with a flashlight, demanding that the ghost he "sensed" show itself. Joey had learned an awful lot from the show over the years. It was also one of the most popular shows on television. Lots of kids from Joey's school watched it, and some of the girls even had pictures of Chris Lopez hanging in their locker.

So why did Joey's interest in ghosts and horror movies make him feel like an outcast?

Because most kids his age had what his mother described as "normal" interests. Even Kevin and Barry sometimes had to be forced into whatever horror-related thing Joey was currently obsessing over—even something as simple as going to see the newest *Big Blood* sequel. And they went along with it for the sake of their friendship, but they just weren't that into that stuff. Instead, Kevin was into every sport imaginable, while Barry was fascinated by the world of pro-wrestling. Joey's other schoolmates shared these same interests—they, too, liked sports and pro-wrestling and superhero comic books. They liked skateboarding and going to the arcade. Except for enjoying them from a distance through their television screens, very few kids were into ghosts and graveyards. It was because of this that Joey was never as popular as the other kids, and this sometimes bothered him. But Chris Lopez—with his shiny, spiked hair and his leather jacket—*he* was cool. And he, too, was into ghosts and monsters and other things Joey was terribly fascinated by. Joey found strength in this, and though he would never willingly admit it to anyone, Chris Lopez was his hero.

On the television, Chris Lopez was stomping up a flight of old, creaky stairs. He paused suddenly and said to the camera, "Did you just hear footsteps?"

Mario wandered in Joey's room, gnawing loudly on a piece of gum and looking around to see if there was something close by he could randomly knock onto the floor—something he often did for no real reason, other than to be an annoying older brother.

"Get out," Joey said, "I'm not in the mood."

"Whoa!" Mario said, dramatically throwing his hands up in the air. "What'd I do?"

"Nothing yet," Joey muttered. "But I know that look. That look means if I leave this room and come back, my Hatchet Harry action figure will be at the bottom of my fish tank."

Mario laughed. "You know me too well, bro." He then grabbed Hatchet Harry off one of Joey's collectible shelves and flipped up the lid of the fish tank.

"Oh, come on!" Joey shouted, and Mario stopped, Hatchet Harry hovering over the fish tank's opening. The television had momentarily stolen his attention.

"Hey, it's that guy," he said, pointing at it with his free hand. "That ghost show guy. What's his name? Chris Loser?"

"Lopez," Joey corrected, rolling his eyes.

"Yeah," Mario said. "He's at the mall today."

"What?" Joey nearly shrieked. "What do you mean?"

"He's at the Bradbury City Mall. He's signing copies of his new book. Douglas told me."

Joey sat straight up in bed, rigid as a corpse. "Chris Lopez is at the Bradbury City Mall?" he bellowed.

"What are you, deaf?" Mario said. "That's what I just said!" He tossed Hatchet Harry into the fish tank and left the bedroom. Harry had barely begun his slow descent to the multicolored rocks at the bottom of tank before Joey was halfway down the stairs.

After ten minutes of begging and promises of chores, Joey was on his way to Bradbury City Mall. As she drove, Mom happily hummed to another song by Dean Martin, who crooned softly along with her on the car stereo.

"Who is this guy you're going to meet again?" Mom asked.

"The coolest guy on P. Earth," Joey answered, almost hopping up and down in his seat. "I love his show and I have all his books. I've wanted to meet him forever. Chris Lopez!"

"Oh, is he the one who teaches you how to make your own bread on those infomercials?" Mom asked

"I have no idea what you're talking about," Joey said. "Please, drive faster! I don't wanna miss him!"

"I'm going as fast as I can, Joey," Mom said, keeping the speedometer at a solid 35 miles per hour.

Joey didn't share this with his mother, but he had other reasons for going other than meeting his idol in person. Ever since coming back from Resurrection Cemetery, a nagging feeling had been planted in Joey's mind and was now festering in his stomach. Everything Joey knew about ghost mythology said that if a person died and was buried in consecrated ground—like a graveyard—then that person should be at peace. And if a person *was* at peace, then their ghost shouldn't be haunting their old house. There had to be some kind of explanation—a reason, or maybe a loophole—why Bob Smah was buried in Resurrection Cemetery, yet still haunting his old house on Creep Street.

And if anyone could tell him how that was possible, it was Chris Lopez.

"Oh, I know who he is. He writes all that bloody monster stuff," Mom continued, her voice tinged in disapproval.

"Sometimes," Joey asked. "But it's all true, though. He doesn't make stuff up."

"Uh huh," Mom said, a little patronizing.

As soon as Joey's mother had located a vacant spot and parked the car, Joey threw open his door and vaulted to the mall's entrance.

"I'll be at the bookstore!" he called over his shoulder.

The mall was packed, as malls usually are on Sundays, and Joey dodged in between crowds of shoppers. He passed by the Halloween costume store, which opened in the mall every September, and he resisted the urge to go in.

He had bigger fish to fry.

Finally he made it to his destination: *Barker's Books.* He stopped when he saw the line of people that began inside the store and continued all the way down the mall and into the food court. Joey sighed with disgust and looked inside the bookstore to confirm that Chris Lopez was, indeed, present as promised.

The fluorescent lights of the store reflected off his spiked hair and Joey's stomach suddenly soared. There he was, in the flesh!

I hope he doesn't think I'm a total loser, Joey thought to himself. Despite the long line, he eagerly took his place at the back, reinvigorated.

The minutes and hours ticked by, and Joey moved closer to the front with each step. His mother had stopped by twice to see if he had made it inside the store yet, and each time she would force a smile and offhandedly mention something else she could go look at, or another store she could shop in. Joey made a mental note to do the chores he had promised her.

His time was soon coming—his feet were now on the carpet of the bookstore. He did his best to calm himself, but it was no easy feat. He was about to meet probably the coolest guy on the planet. Who *wouldn't* be nervous?

"Next!" said a voice. Joey turned, his eyes wide, like a deer caught in headlights. A pretty blonde girl stood before him; she was dressed in black and wearing a *Spooky Mysteries* ID tag around her neck. She handed Joey a hardcover book and he looked down at it. Chris Lopez was on the cover, his arm around the shoulder of a skeleton wearing a suit. The book was called *Bones and Blood: My Spooky Life*.

Joey gazed up in awe, everything suddenly droning to slow motion. Chris Lopez sat before him behind a table. He grinned.

"What's up, little dude?" he asked and held up his hand for a high-five. Joey only stared back, suddenly forgetting how to speak.

"I..." Joey began and then said nothing.

Chris laughed. "Come on, dude, I'm not the president. I chase ghosts!"

"I know!" Joey finally said. "That's so much cooler!"

Chris laughed again and Joey finally slapped him five. He handed Chris the book, and the spiky-haired ghost-chaser opened it and grabbed a black pen from a pile on the table. "What's your name, little dude?" he asked.

"Um...Joe...y. Um, just make it out to Joe. Or, Joey is fine. Whatever, you know, I—"

Chris grinned at Joey's nervousness and scrawled something in the book. Once done, he enthusiastically slid it across the table to Joey, who caught it eagerly and read the inscription.

To Joe(y)! Watch out for spooks! – Chris Lopez!

"Wow," Joey said, letting an awed gasp escape his mouth. He had never before seen an exclamation point placed at the end of someone's name, but for some reason, it seemed right at home following the name of Chris Lopez.

"Enjoy the book, little dude!" his hero declared.

But Joey did not move. Instead, he leaned in a little closer. "Mr. Lopez...do you believe that if the body of a person is buried, the spirit is at rest?"

"Sure, little bro," Chris said, nodding. "Of all the ghost stories I've ever heard, or haunted places I've ever investigated, most of them were based on someone having died, but their body not having been properly buried."

Joey nodded. "What about those other times when the body was buried, and the ghost continued to exist? What was keeping them here, if not their body?"

"That's what I call unfinished business," Chris said. "That's when something beyond the spirit's physical body is keeping them here."

"What do you mean by 'something'? Like, an object?"

Chris mischievously winked at him. "Sounds like a good place to start!"

An object! That's what's keeping Bob's spirit here!

Finally, Joey felt one step closer!

"Thanks, Mr. Lopez!" Joey shouted, grateful.

"You got it, little dude," Chris said and held up his palm again. Joey slapped it and Chris grinned his pearly-white teeth. "Enjoy the book!"

Joey nodded and smiled. He was ushered to another line where he paid for his book, and then walked out of the store. The people still waiting in line nervously chattered and laughed, but Joey did not hear them. They were nothing more than a muddied sea of noise in the back of his mind. He walked to a nearby bench and sat down, his new book in a bag hanging loosely from his fingers.

Joey closed his eyes and mentally searched the Smah house, trying to visualize every nook and cranny of the structure. He had seen so many things inside the house—so many random objects. Which one was keeping Bob Smah from resting in peace? And further, was it even in the house? Maybe it wasn't! Maybe it was sold at a yard sale, or thrown away, or a hundred other things that could have happened!

Joey came to Chris Lopez looking for answers—looking to feel one step closer to helping Bob Smah rest in peace. And Chris had given him the answer he was seeking. At first it had felt like a revelation, but the more Joey thought about it, he realized he was still unsatisfied—now more than ever.

CHAPTER TEN

"Don't you think there's a chance it was just your imagination?" Barry asked.

Barry and Joey were sitting on Joey's front porch in the mid-afternoon. Joey had called Barry as soon as he had gotten home from the bookstore, and now the two were discussing the ghostly goings-on at Creep Street.

"Like, remember that time we watched the *Dr. Strangles* marathon at Kevin's house, and the whole walk home that night we were convinced Dr. Strangles was somewhere out there watching us and getting ready to strangle?" Barry continued.

"It would be so much easier if I could just believe that," Joey said, sighing. "What I saw seemed so real, though. Besides, after what Michael told us, and everything we've learned…"

"I read that one Chris Lopez book you made me borrow," Barry said, "and it said that we sometimes leave energy in the places we inhabit. And if there is a violent or bad event, more energy is left over, sort of like a fingerprint left behind. Maybe that's what's happening in that house:

something tragic happened there, and it just gives off bad vibes."

Joey took this in, wanting to put his full belief behind this theory, but it did nothing for him. "I wish we hadn't gone in that house," he finally said. "It was a stupid idea, and all because I wanted—"

Joey stopped suddenly, his hand going to his face. He groaned, feeling immediately stupid.

"Wanted what?" Barry asked.

Joey couldn't even look his friend in the eye when he said, "I figured if I could get you guys to go inside that house for a cheap thrill, you'd see that stuff like that was still fun. And maybe you would've given trick-or-treating another chance…"

"Oh," Barry said, also feeling embarrassed, as he recalled his recent shame in letting down his friend.

"I wish *that* was my biggest problem right now: you guys not wanting to go trick-or-treating anymore," Joey admitted.

Both boys were silent for a moment.

"You know what," Barry began, "you need a distraction from all this ghoulish stuff. Let's go costume shopping!"

Joey smiled slightly. "I thought you guys were too *cool* for Halloween?"

"Yeah, well, Kevin can go suck some eggs," Barry said. "If he doesn't want to trick-or-treat, that means more candy for me."

"And me!" Joey said.

They rode their bikes to Irwin's Hardware and looked through the Halloween costume section. Rows and rows of pre-packaged costumes and hideous, grinning masks awaited them.

"Joey, check it out!" Barry said. Joey turned around to see Barry holding up a large novelty derriere. He put it on his forehead. Joey cracked up and shook his head.

The boys spent over an hour in the store, trying on masks and making each other laugh. Barry put on a particularly elaborate Frankenstein's Monster mask that was too big for him, and as a result, he walked right into a wall.

Eventually, Mr. Irwin yelled at them. "Are you two gonna buy something or not?"

"It's quite possible," Joey said.

Barry comically reached into his pockets and pulled out their fabric, signaling he was very broke.

Joey laughed. "Spend all your money at Chickens Lickens again?"

Barry blushed, but tried to smile through it.

"Come back once you have some money!" Mr. Irwin barked.

The boys walked out of the store, trying to stifle their giggling.

As they walked home, the sun was starting to set, bringing Sunday to a close—always the worst time for young boys who wanted nothing more than to never have to deal with school again. However, Joey took comfort in knowing that even though another school week was upon them, it was bringing Halloween with it.

Halloween—the day he waited for all year.

And yet, this year was different. And not just because of Kevin's sudden self-proclaimed maturity—which was laughable, especially coming from a kid who hid a book of dirty jokes under his mattress. No, there was that lousy house on Creep Street to contend with.

And like that, a mental image of the place suddenly flooded his mind again. Joey couldn't believe it, but he had managed to completely forget about the house while he and Barry had been messing around in the store. But now it was seeping back into his thoughts, and it gave him a queasy feeling in his stomach.

"I better get inside," Barry said, glancing at his house. "My dad will tan my hide if I'm late for hot dog night."

"Okay, man," Joey said. "See you at school tomorrow."

"Ugh, don't remind me," Barry said. "Mac McDonaldson is looking to punch me in the nose because I wouldn't let him cheat off my biology test on Friday." He waved goodbye and went inside.

I better get home too, Joey thought. However, though he could see his house from where he was, he found himself turning around and riding in the opposite direction.

Where are you going, Joey? he thought as he pedaled his bike down empty, leaf-scattered streets.

Nowhere. It's just a nice night, just taking the long way home...

People had begun lighting their jack-o-lanterns and their carved faces glowed eerily in the twilight.

You're not going where I think you're going, are you, Joey?

"No, sir," he said out loud. "No way, no how."

But before long, he came upon the faded green street sign marked *CREEP STREET.*

The sky was darkening at a rapid pace. The air grew brisker.

Joey pulled up in front of the Smah house. It looked even more ominous now, in that time just between light and dark. Because it was more visible than in the full-on night, and it looked bigger somehow; as if it had grown since he'd seen it last.

Whatever you do, do NOT go in that house alone.

"Wouldn't think of it," Joey said to himself, letting his bike fall to the cool grass. Ignoring the foreboding voice in his mind, he walked right toward the front door.

Didn't you promise Dad you wouldn't mess around with this place anymore?

But the house was pulling him in. His desire to know if he had really seen a ghost was simply too powerful; it was controlling him now.

I won't stay long, he whispered to himself as he turned the rusty doorknob and pushed open the door on its creaking hinges. *Just a few minutes, and if I don't see anything, then I'll know it was all in my head. And I can finally move on and forget about this place.*

Joey looked up and down the empty street, hoping that maybe someone was there to see him…and stop him. But the street was a barren wasteland.

He stepped into the darkness of the house. The smell of mold and dust hit him, making him feel as if he were going to sneeze.

"Hello?" he called out. "Anyone in here?"

Silence.

He left the front door open and stepped deeper into the house—into what must have been the living room. The furniture was still there, like it had been a couple nights ago, and it was still covered in dusty white sheets. An ancient-looking television sat in a corner, its screen smashed in.

I bet there are rats in this place, he thought, then shook the thought away.

"Well!" Joey said, clapping his hands together. "Nothing to see. Time to go."

Don't you want to look upstairs, buddy? That's where you saw the hand, after all.

"I think I'll pass," Joey told himself, but without even realizing what he was doing, he began walking up that creaking staircase, clouds of dust rising up with each footfall. Joey, inwardly, knew that this was all a bad idea. Being in this house with two of his friends *and* his brother had been creepy enough—but being in it now by himself?

But he couldn't resist it. He was impulsive by nature—sometimes too impulsive for his own good. When his mind was taken hostage by crazy theories and ideas, there was no denying himself. His reason would shut down, and his body would carry out these phantom orders. As increasingly terrified as Joey was growing, he was determined to find out once and for all if there really was a ghost in this house. The desire was too compelling to resist.

He climbed the stairs into nearly pitch darkness; there were no windows in the upstairs hallways, and even if there had been, the sun had long set behind the horizon. He took out a small flashlight he had on his keychain and unleashed its tiny beam. The light did not help much, but it was better than being in total blackness.

He looked down the hallway he had explored his previous time in the house—more specifically at the door where that ghostly white finger had appeared. Only this time, now with the aid of his tiny light, he saw a crude, hand-shaped sign hanging on the door—a sign declaring *BOB'S ROOM.*

"I'm not going in there," Joey said. "I can't."

And at last, his body obeyed. He made no movement toward the room. Instead, he tried a door closer to him. It swung open quickly after he turned the knob, causing him to jump back, startled. The awaiting room was small, and there were several items throughout, also covered in white sheets. Joey deduced it must have been a storage room at some point; he could make out distinctive shapes of lamps and chairs and tables under the sheets. There was a small oval window in the room, and through it, the moon shone bright and full like a glowing skull.

Okay, Joey, you've satisfied your morbid curiosity. You've been here for at least five minutes and no ghoulies have jumped out at you. It's time to go home.

Joey turned to leave, and then he froze. He was positive one of the sheet-covered items in the corner had moved.

"H-hello?" he whispered, his voice sounding tiny.

Your mind is playing tricks on you. That sheet did NOT move. Time to GO.

The sheet moved again. A slight flutter, but it definitely moved.

Joey felt his heart pounding in his chest. It was pounding so loudly that he could hear it. He needed to get out of there. Now. But he was frozen in place, as if someone had glued his sneakers to the dusty floorboards.

He swallowed and spoke up.

"I…I want to help you. I know that you died here, and I want to help…I want to help you find peace."

He was shivering all over. His hand shook violently and the small beam of light from his flashlight seized.

The sheet was flung away, and out from under it stepped Bob Smah.

Joey wanted to scream; everything inside him told him to scream. But his mouth merely hung open, and no sound escaped.

Bob no longer looked like the boy Joey and his friends had seen in the home movies or the photographs. His face was dry and decayed, his lips peeled away showing tiny white teeth. His whole body glowed with an otherworldly light, and his movements were jerky and unnatural. He did not move like a thing from this world, because he was *not* from this world—this thing in the corner was not human. And the worst part was his eyes—or lack thereof. Bob did not have eyes in the grinning, fleshy skull that was his head.

Instead he had two deep black orbs, and deep in the orbs, as if from a small fire within, two tiny white dots glowed.

"You want to help?" Bob asked. His voice was scratchy and distant, as if it were coming from an old record player on a wax cylinder recorded many years ago. "And how can you...help me?" The ghost boy advanced on Joey, his inhuman, jerking movements sending shivers up and down Joey's spine. "How can you help...the dead?" he asked, and began laughing—a sickening, childlike laughter.

That laughter broke the spell holding Joey captive, and he turned and ran. The laughter grew louder and harsher as he ran down the stairs and out the front door. He grabbed his bike, jumped on, and took off. He could still hear the laughter, all the way down the block, all the way to his own house.

He threw his bike on the lawn, ran into his house, sprinted up the steps without saying a word to anyone, and buried himself under the covers of his bed.

He would not find sleep that night.

Joey's mind whirred a mile a minute. There were so many thoughts, and each of them flashed an eerie image of the lone house—of its crippled front door, its dusty corners...and its monstrous occupant.

It was actually real—Bob Smah haunted the house on Creep Street. And though Joey was terrified by what he had seen—by a ghost who had likely perfected scaring people away from his home for years—Joey *had* to do something about it. But he couldn't do it alone. He *wouldn't* do it alone, not after what he had just experienced. He had to convince his friends to help him, somehow.

Bob's words rang in his head: "How can you help…the dead?"

Joey didn't know, but he had to find a way.

* * *

The old caretaker checked his watch and saw that it was approaching midnight. He stood up shakily from his rickety wooden stool, wondering where the day had gone. His mind had wandered again—and it wasn't the first time. It had been happening for years, but it was definitely getting worse. His mind often wandered and dreamed of the past—of the days he was happy, and when things seemed like they might work out.

He slid his timecard into the ancient clock and its stamp rang out with a heavy metal thud, like a cash register drawer slamming shut, and he let the withered card fall down to the small cramped desk. He eyed his cot behind him in the next room, considered spending the night there instead, but then decided against it. He stepped out of his small office and shut the door behind him, locking it with one of the many keys on his ancient key ring. He did the same thing with the large impressive front cemetery gates, slowly closing them with a squeal and locking them with another key—this one more antiquated.

He then set off to the cemetery's back exit, where he would lock the gate behind him, and head home to the house he shared with no one. As he walked, he passed many names, long etched on stones.

People he had known in his life.

By an old, near-dead oak tree sat the grave of Gary Miller, a good man who had died in the late 1950s. Buried next to him was his wife, Maggie, who had never re-married. The Millers were together in death as they had been in life.

A few graves over, the old caretaker saw the final resting place of Patricia Sherlock, an older woman who had died at her home of a heart attack. Her cemetery plot, which had been pre-bought as far back as the 1960s, had sat vacant for years, awaiting her inevitable end. Though she had died five or so years ago—it was the last grave the old man had managed to dig on his own before having to hire a lazy, part-time youth with a smart mouth. The part-timer had dug all the graves since—the old man was too ancient to do so himself. His role of gravedigger had become caretaker, which meant that unless he was chasing out unruly kids after hours, or cleaning up dead grave blankets, he sat on a stool and let time pass. And as he sat, he thought about all the mistakes in his life. They haunted him like a ghost, never letting him have a single day of peace. If anyone had ever bothered to speak to him in a social manner, they would easily see how sad he was. But that was not a risk—no one ever spoke to him at all.

The old caretaker continued his hobbling walk, and as he did so, passed the Smah plot. His heart ached suddenly, and that familiar feeling of overwhelming sadness took him again. Seeing the stone bearing their names—an entire family whose lives were taken much before their time—forced him to reflect on his own life.

If only I could do it all again, the old caretaker thought. *I would do it differently. I would be a better person. Oh, how long must a person live with their sins before it ends them?*

His shoulders drooped, his eyes wet, he continued his trek to the back gate, feeling surrounded by ghosts of the past, as well as demons of his own. He made it to the back exit and stepped out, closing the gate behind him and locking it up tight. He cast another tired glance into the dark cemetery before climbing into his ancient pick-up truck and setting off on his short trip home.

As he drove, the old caretaker found himself going out of his way. Winding down side streets, the truck—almost as old as he was—bouncing and creaking. He found himself taking a left onto a street he never, ever wanted to set foot on again: Creep Street.

The street was empty and dead, filled with nothing but dirt lots and rusted fences hanging on their last leg. He tightened his grip on the steering wheel and slowed the truck to a crawl. His headlights cut beams across the darkness, and there, at the end of the street, were the remains of the Smah house.

The old caretaker killed his headlights and sat, looking at the empty home. He remembered the boy who had once lived there—and who had died there as well. He had gotten so used to seeing the boy's name scrawled across his tombstone—a sign that he had died—that seeing this house before him—a sign that the boy had also once lived—filled him with strange feelings.

He was suddenly shaken from his melancholy when the front door of the house flew open and a boy came running out. The boy grabbed a nearby discarded bike and rode like lightning right past the truck, never looking back. It took the old man's failing eyes a moment, but he recognized the boy: it was one of the three meddling kids who had come to his cemetery earlier in the week, looking for the Smah graves. And now the boy had been trespassing in the Smah house.

Can't these kids leave well enough alone? Can't they let the Smahs rest in peace?

The old caretaker turned off the truck engine and climbed out of the cab. The front door of the Smah house still hung open.

Better close it, he thought, his caretaking instincts taking over. *Close it so no more kids get in there and disturb the dead.*

Up onto the porch he went. He was about to shut the door when he heard something from within the bowels of the darkened house. He stiffened, and felt his withered heart begin to thud in his chest.

Just an old house, he thought. *Old houses make sounds…*

But the sound came again, and he recognized it for what it was: the sound of a child giggling.

Maybe one of that boy's two friends are still in the house, up to no good.

But deep down, he knew that wasn't the case. There was something *off* about that giggling.

The old caretaker took a few steps into the house, the smell of dust and decay hitting him almost instantly. He heard footsteps thudding around upstairs—someone running.

"Who's in here?" he called out, his voice hoarse.

Sudden silence filled the house—an eerie, abnormal silence. The old caretaker's heart was pounding even faster now. He looked up the stairs and he saw a figure leaning over the bannister above: the figure of a small boy.

"You kids get outta here!" the old caretaker cried.

The giggling came again; horrible and bloodcurdling. The shape on the landing above slowly moved in an unnatural manner, and the old caretaker heard a voice whisper, directly in his ear:

Why should I get out? This is MY house…

The old caretaker slowly turned and saw that the figure was no longer upstairs, but now directly next to him. It was bathed in shadow, but its eyes glowed, like some wild animal caught in the beams of headlights.

The old caretaker ran from the house, as fast as his aching legs could take him. His heart was pounding furiously now; he could hear his own pulse throbbing in his ears.

He made it home, finally, and sat in the dark of his one-bedroom apartment, located above the hardware store. He poured himself a drink, hoping to calm down. But his heart wouldn't slow, and his body wouldn't stop shaking. He drank and drank until everything started to fade.

ONE DAY TILL HALLOWEEN

CHAPTER ELEVEN

Joey stared hard at the ceiling of his bedroom, his covers clutched tightly under his chin, until light from the rising sun chased away the dark of the night and the awful presence of Bob Smah. It wasn't until he heard Dad banging around and getting ready for work that he felt safe enough to get out of bed. He jumped into a pair of wrinkled jeans and an Acres of Rage official band t-shirt and walked down the steps.

"Joey, you're up early," Dad said, his head hung low over a bowl of oatmeal. "So am I. Just like every single day of my life."

"Dad," Joey began and sat down at the table. His words escaped him then. He had no idea how to even begin asking his father about ghosts and haunted houses and murder—and further, how to handle such issues.

"What's up, sport? Is it geometry again? You know I'd help you if I could, but I'm no good at that stuff. I passed geometry by fixing my teacher's radiator."

"How do you help someone who doesn't want to be helped?" Joey blurted out.

Dad slid the spoon down his bowl for another scoop of his horse-food breakfast. "Who needs help?"

"Just a boy I know."

"Is it serious?"

"Pretty serious, yeah."

Dad put down his spoon, wiped his mouth, and looked at his son. "Who is it?"

"I...can't tell you."

"Why not?"

Joey waited a moment, searching for a believable lie. "I promised him I wouldn't tell anyone."

Dad nodded. "Remember that time your uncle was sick, but he wouldn't go see the doctor?"

Joey nodded. His Uncle Bart was known for being incredibly stubborn—and for not trusting anyone. Especially doctors.

"Well, do you remember what happened next?" Dad continued. "He refused and refused to go until I called the doctor for him and had him pay your uncle a visit. And once he examined your uncle, the doctor found out he had pneumonia. Who knows what would have happened to him if I hadn't stepped in?"

Joey nodded. "I remember."

"You can always help a person, Joey; whether they want your help or not. Even if you try to help someone and you fail, it at least shows you cared enough to try. Sometimes, that's help enough. Understand?"

"I think so," Joey said. "Thanks."

Dad bent to him. "C'mon, who is it? You can tell your old man. Is it Kevin?"

"No," Joey said.

"Are you trying to make the kid take more showers?"

Joey smiled a little, despite himself.

"Because he smells like a truck stop?"

Joey laughed and he covered his mouth before he could disturb the other Tonellis, who were still sound asleep. "I'll tell you what, Dad: if I can give my friend the help he needs, I promise I'll tell you all about it."

"Deal," Dad said. He ruffled Joey's hair once and picked up his tool bag from another kitchen chair. "Hey, it's Halloween tomorrow, ain't it?"

Joey nodded, his face briefly perking up before the reminder of Bob Smah quickly chased away his enthusiasm.

"Did you save any of your allowance for a costume?"

"I did," Joey said, "but then I bought a book instead. It kinda wiped me out."

Dad fished around in his pocket and withdrew a bundle of cash—not encased in a wallet, but wrapped in a rubber band. He refused to use a wallet, even when the kids had bought him one as a Christmas gift. They had long given up trying to figure out why.

Dad handed Joey a few wrinkled bills. "Buy something really scary this year," he said, smiling at his son.

"Thanks, Dad," Joey said, earnestly grateful. "For everything."

Dad walked out the front door and Joey could hear him crunching over the gravel driveway on his way to his work van.

Joey's mind began working again. Between what Chris Lopez and Dad had told him, he had a rough idea of how to help Bob Smah. The only problem was, he couldn't do it alone—no way.

As Joey climbed the stairs back to his room to get ready for school, he rehearsed in his mind exactly what he needed to say to Barry and Kevin.

CHAPTER TWELVE

Kevin walked through the halls of Mary Shelley Middle School, his hands in the pockets of his jeans, his lucky ball cap on backwards.

Girls at their lockers turned to him and smiled nervously.

"Hi, Kevin," said Mable Sachs, blushing.

"What's up, babe?" Kevin asked, shooting his finger at her like a gun.

"Good morning, Kevin!" said Jenny Jumper, and then she giggled.

"See *you* in history, Jenny," Kevin said and winked at her. She swooned.

Kevin didn't usually see Barry and Joey at school until third period, which was study hall. Barry and Joey, however, were in the same homeroom. During second period, while Kevin was at gym class, Barry had walked by the door to the gymnasium and handed him a note.

"Gotta go," Barry had said quickly. "Being this close to the gym makes me nervous."

Kevin had read the note after class, which said:

Kevin,
Don't go to study hall. Meet me in the theater.
- Joey.

Kevin looked at the note, confused, but at the same time, he wasn't that surprised. He had definitely noticed Joey acting really strange lately—and on edge. And granted, Joey had always been a *little* strange, but this latest ghost stuff had gotten out of hand. Ever since they were little kids, Joey had always been obsessed with monster movies and creepy stuff. He had often made the friends watch hour after hour of mindless movies that featured maniacs with chainsaws cutting off the legs of screaming teens. Kevin and Barry sort of liked those movies, too, but Joey took it to a whole new level. He had once spent fifty dollars to buy a toy designed to look like his favorite horror movie slasher, Big Blood! That was extreme—Kevin generally spent his money on new baseball bats or dirty joke books.

Still, weird or not, Joey was a friend, so if he wanted to have a mysterious secret meeting, Kevin would oblige.

* * *

Barry was going to be late.

After his biology class ended, he had stayed behind to talk to Dr. Bookman about their experiment—dissecting owl puke. Most of the other kids in class had been grossed out, but Barry had loved it. He had even found a tiny mouse skull in the puke!

"Isn't this awesome?" he had asked, holding the skull up to Susie Sampkins.

"Ewwww! Get away!" she had shrieked.

Barry had always liked science—specifically biology. He was fascinated by animals and plants, and how they could adapt to their own environments. And though the students of Mary Shelley Middle School would have to wait until high school to begin taking classes on chemistry and physics, that didn't stop Barry from reading about those subjects on his own time. He was especially fascinated by the Modern Theory of Matter, which stated that, since everything in the universe was comprised of matter, everything was, therefore, connected. Barry found that very comforting, though he couldn't put into words why.

But that didn't mean Barry loved *everything* made of matter. After all, next week Dr. Bookman was going to have the class dissect rats. Barry *hated* rats, and not just because he was terrified of them.

While talking with Dr. Bookman about the owl puke, Barry had suddenly remembered the friends' meeting in the theater and run from the room in mid-sentence.

Barry was worried about Joey, too. His friend had come into homeroom that morning looking exhausted; big, dark circles under his eyes and his hair a mess. "I have to talk to both of you," he had whispered, handing him a piece of paper. "Find Kevin and give him this note. When it's time for study hall, meet me in the theater."

"Is everything okay?" Barry had asked.

"I don't know," had been Joey's reply.

Barry was now moving quickly through the halls. He reached the doors to the school theater at the exact moment Kevin arrived, much to his relief

"Oh good, I thought I was late," Barry said, out of breath.

"What's up, Barrman?" Kevin asked. "What's with mysterious Joey's mysterious note of mystery?"

"I guess we'll find out," Barry answered, shrugging.

They pushed open the doors and entered. The theater was dark. There were small lights lining the aisles, and the stage itself was lit with dim overhead bulbs. They did not see their friend.

"Joey?" Kevin called out, his voice echoing. They walked down the aisle and up the stairs that led to the stage, looking around. It appeared to be empty.

"Joey, where are you?" Barry yelled.

"Up here," came a reply. Barry and Kevin gasped and looked up. Joey was above them, standing on a catwalk above the stage. "Come up. I don't want anyone to know we're in here."

Up on the catwalk, there was a small wall above the railing. It was littered with graffiti from other students; things like: *Mr. Adams Sucks; Mable Sachs Smells Like A Mule;* and one written in bright red pen that said: *Larry Jerry Lives.*

"What's up, dude?" Kevin asked Joey as the three boys stood side by side on the catwalk.

"I went back to the house on Creep Street last night," Joey confessed.

"Alone?" Barry gasped.

"Joey, I think you should go see Dr. Sally," Kevin said. "You're acting bonkers."

"I don't need the school shrink. I need you guys to help me," Joey went on. "To come with me to the house and try to help this ghost once and for all. And believe me, there *is* a ghost, and it *is* Bob Smah. I saw him last night."

"Joey, no," Barry whispered. "We can't go back there. Maybe Kevin is right. You've been acting really weird."

Kevin nodded.

Joey sighed. "I thought long and hard about how I was going to convince you guys to come back with me to the house," he said, looking over the railing down at the stage. "I thought of a million reasons. I even thought of a few lies. But it comes down to this."

Joey turned around and faced his friends. "Barry, remember when you stood in line all night to get those

WrestleTime tickets, and your parents or sister didn't want to wait with you? Who waited with you that whole night?"

Barry blushed. "You and Kevin…"

"And Kevin," Joey continued, "do you remember when spring training was coming up for little league, and you had no one to help you train? No one to pitch to you and play outfield? What happened then?"

Kevin nodded. "You guys did it…"

"We're friends, guys," Joey said. "And that means something. Friends can be a dime a dozen to some people, but not to me. There's nothing I wouldn't do for you guys. I know what I'm asking you to do is a much bigger deal than fielding baseballs or standing in line, but, I'm still asking you right now to be a friend to me—to help me…because this is something I have to do. And I'll do it with or without you. But I would much rather have you guys by my side."

Barry looked down at his sneakers. Kevin sighed and rubbed the back of his head with his hand.

"I'm in," Barry said. "You know I'm in."

Barry and Joey looked at Kevin, who shrugged. "What the heck? I can't let you two idiots have all the fun."

Joey felt the tension vanish from his shoulders. Relief washed over him. At first he'd been apprehensive about hearing his friends' reactions to his request. But now, standing before the two of them, he felt guilty for ever having doubted their loyalty.

"So, when are we going?" Kevin asked.

"Tomorrow night," Joey said, his words echoing off the walls of the theater. "Halloween."

CHAPTER THIRTEEN

Joey had gone home after school feeling incredibly elated. He was intent on staring death in the face on Halloween night, despite how terrified that thought made him, but knowing his friends would be by his side somehow made it a little more bearable.

His moment of elation quickly vanished when he opened the front door and saw his father—furious and waiting for him at the kitchen table. Loud yelling quickly followed.

"You promised me that you wouldn't go into that house!" Dad bellowed. Joey could always tell when his father was at his angriest, because his weird, M-shaped vein bulged over one of his temples.

"I'm sorry, Dad," was all Joey could say. And it was true: he *had* promised his father he wouldn't go into the house, but he had broken that promise. He didn't feel entirely guilty, though—his father had enforced that promise assuming that Joey was up to no good and walking around an abandoned house for the fun of it. If Dad had known what was *really* going on in that house—and what was at stake—Joey was sure he wouldn't have been nearly as angry.

"That place is who-knows how old—maybe a hundred years!" Dad continued. "It's way too dangerous for you to be playing around in there!"

"We weren't playing!" Joey defended.

"Oh, I know," Dad said, scoffing. "You were *ghost hunting*. Michael told me *all* about it."

Mom rolled her eyes behind Joey's father and mouthed Michael's name in disgust.

"But there really is—" Joey began.

"Spare me!" Dad shouted, cutting him off. "A little boy died there, and you're treating it like a playground!" His yelling subsided, but his anger did not. "I am so furious with you I can't even see straight. I'm tempted to throw out all your monster diorama stuff."

"Dear, please," intervened Mom, the usual voice of reason. "Joey has always been good and done whatever we asked him to do. Maybe we shouldn't be so hard on him about this."

"He *promised* me," Dad said, cocking his thumb against his chest. "Looked right in my eyes and promised me! *That's* why I'm so upset!"

"But Dad, I had to go in there!" Joey cried. "You have to believe me! There really is a ghost in there, and he needs my help!"

Mario, who had been monitoring the argument from the entranceway to the kitchen, laughed out loud.

"Go clean your room," Dad barked at him.

"I just cleaned it yesterday!" Mario responded.

"Then go clean *my* room!" Dad growled back at him.

Mario threw up his arms in defeat and walked away.

Dad whipped his head over at Joey again. "You know, I'm *this* close to grounding you for tomorrow—meaning no trick-or-treating."

Joey's mouth dropped open. He was about to protest his father's threat, but his mother spoke up again.

"Dear, is that really necessary? You know how excited he's been about trick-or-treating. Let's not be hasty."

Dad exhaled heavily, and Joey felt slight relief. He was quiet for a long time, staring at the kitchen floor, his arms crossed.

Mom's pleads seemed to have done the trick.

"Joey, listen to me," Dad finally said and grasped his son's arms. "I cannot make this any more clear. You are to never, ever, go back into that house, ever again. Not ever. Is that clear? Is it finally sinking in?"

Joey cast a saddened glance down to the ground. "Yes, sir," he said.

"Good," he said, straightening and walking away. "I'll be in the garage. Call me for dinner. " He walked out of the house.

Joey turned and looked at his mother. "Thanks, Mom."

She smiled a crooked smile at him. "Don't make me regret sticking my neck out for you, okay? Don't go into that house again."

Joey nodded, and Mom turned her attention back to the stove, where she was preparing that night's dinner. He ran up to his room, past his parents' room where Mario was vacuuming, and shut his door.

He dialed Barry's number, and as he waited for him to pick up, he couldn't help but feel guilty.

Because he had no choice but to defy his parents' wishes…one more time.

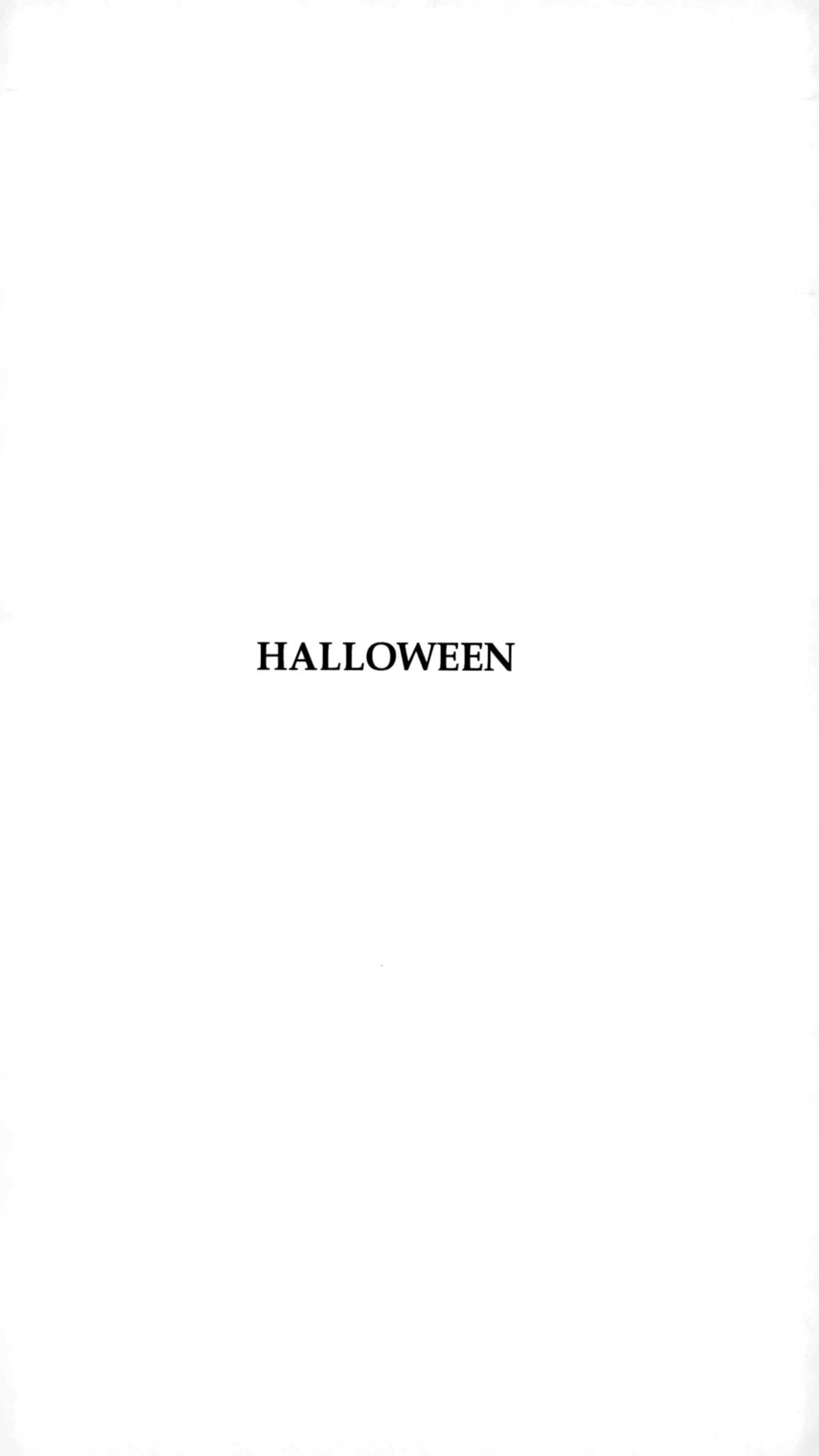

HALLOWEEN

CHAPTER FOURTEEN

As the hour struck midnight, the dust in the house on Creep Street began to stir. The floorboards creaked loudly, and wind whistled through the cracks in chilling screams.

Bob Smah—the lone, ghostly inhabitant of his former earthly home—knew the day well. He knew it better than any other day of the year.

October 31st.

Halloween.

It was the day Bob's physical body had ceased to be. It was the day the bullies had finally caught up with him.

Thinking back on his life, Bob knew that everything began to go wrong after his father's death. His mother, who had always been prone to what she described as "bad patches," had slowly begun to lose her mind. Her strange behavior in public had become the talk of the small town. In a small town, gossip thrived, because everybody knew everybody, and you couldn't help but be curious about what went on behind closed doors. The gossip about "crazy Betty Smah" had made its way to the schoolyard, and a merciless gang of bullies, who proudly went by the nickname "The

Terrible Trio," had set their sights on Bob. He was made to suffer for his mother's uncontrollable illness.

There was Randall "Tough" Buggins, the leader of the gang. He was the oldest kid in Bob's grade, due to the fact that he had been left back three times thanks to his terrible grades. And always accompanying him was Wendell Lane, who under different circumstances would've been bullied himself, with his slight frame, thick glasses, and bad complexion. But Wendell was a bit of a brainiac, and he let Tough cheat off his papers, and this was enough to earn his way into Tough's inner circle. And then there was Ralph Gardner, who never quite seemed like he belonged in the Terrible Trio. He was a quiet kid, broad-shouldered with mean looking eyes. He had a temper and was prone to random bouts of anger, but once anyone got to know him they could see that he really wasn't that bad—that he just ran with the wrong crowd.

The Terrible Trio ruled Mary Shelley Middle School back in Bob Smah's day, and if you happened to be on their radar, your life became miserable. Deep down, Bob had known it was only a matter of time—once stories about his mother's strange behavior became common knowledge—before the three bullies would turn their wrath on him. And once they did, they were brutal. Not a day went by when they weren't heckling or berating him. On several occasions,

Tough had cornered Bob in the boys' bathroom and stuck his head in the toilet.

What made the whole thing extra unbearable was the fact that Bob had no one he could turn to. Going to teachers would instantly label him a snitch, which was something no kid wanted to be. And as for Bob's mother, the last thing he wanted to do was add to her sorrow by telling her all about his problems. So he was forced to take it. He was small for his age, and there was no chance of ever really being able to fight back.

One day, Bob had been playing by himself in Lovecraft Memorial Park, and the Trio had spotted him. Tough had held him down while Wendell dumped clumps of sand all over Bob's face. Bob had kicked and squirmed and called for help, but it was no use. And the entire time it went on, Ralph had stood in the background, his arms crossed, a frown on his face. Bob had looked into Ralph's eyes, pleading with him to help. And for the briefest of moments, Bob could've sworn he saw real sympathy and pity in Ralph's eyes. Ralph had opened his mouth, as if he were going to put a stop to it. But instead he said, "What you lookin' at, cry baby?" He had then turned his back on the entire miserable sight and went off to carve his name in a nearby oak tree with the pocketknife he always carried.

Bob came home from school weekly with fresh bruises, and his mother, lost in her own illness, hadn't even noticed. It had all been too much, and one day Bob had finally broken down, sobbing uncontrollably and telling his mother all about it. His mother was heartbroken. She felt ashamed that she had not noticed how terrible things were for him. She promised him that things were going to change—that things were going to get better. She started going to a doctor—one located in Bradbury, outside of Blackwood, to keep the rumors away. And one day she had marched over to Tough Buggins' house, wearing her prettiest sundress and her angriest look. Tough's father, who hadn't worked in over a year since his "accident" down at the shipyard in the city, had answered the door, a can of beer in his hand and a smug look on his face.

"Well, if it ain't the town nut-job," he had said.

"Yes," Betty Smah had said, her hands on her hips. "And if it ain't the town drunk."

"What did you say to me, lady?" Tough's father had barked.

"Shut your ignorant mouth, Mr. Buggins," Betty had said. "I may be the town nut-job, and I may be just some poor, defenseless woman, but my husband was a hero. He was twice the man you are, and three times the man that little bully son of yours will ever be. So you tell him that if he lays another hand on my boy—who, I might add, is not even half the size your *large* boy is—there's gonna be trouble. After all,

I'm the town nut-job. Who knows what *crazy* thing I might do?"

Betty Smah had marched away, her head held high. And since talk had a way of spreading in Blackwood, it wasn't long before the entire town had heard what she'd done. There was no love in town for the Buggins family, and people had actually been downright proud of Betty for standing up for her boy. And Mr. Buggins became even more of a laughing stock, having been put in his place by a *woman*. It even seemed to work—the Terrible Trio had left Bob alone.

At least, for a while.

And then Halloween came, and Tough had decided to get even with the Smahs. He hadn't much cared to be the focus of other kids' jokes and comments—about how a *mom* had gotten the better of both him and his father. He couldn't let that go by. He had rallied up Wendell and Ralph and headed over to the Smah house, each of them carrying pillow sacks loaded up with eggs and toilet paper. They didn't really have a plan other than to "mess up the place." But everything changed when they found out Bob was home alone.

And as for what happened next, only Bob and the bullies know—and they were *all* dead now.

Though Bob was dead, his awareness continued to exist. He had his thoughts and memories; his pain and anger. They so often drifted back and forth that one moment he could be floating through his empty home, sad from his isolation, but then anger would surge through him and he would wish for nothing but death for all that had ever wronged him—especially his parents for leaving him. It was because of this awareness that he felt like an old soul. His deformed body may have suggested an age of twelve, but his mind was much older, much more mature. After all, he'd had nothing but time to wallow around his empty house; and before that, to observe his mother in her grief following his death; to learn about mourning and loss. He didn't feel twelve—not at all. He felt one hundred. Because in a way, he was.

He looked out the window of his home and down to Creep Street below. The dark holes that were once his eyes narrowed at the quiet street. His block had once been littered with many houses, all filled with friendly neighbors and bright futures. But now the houses were gone, and the people long dead. His house was the sole remaining structure, and it deepened his isolation.

Bob was aware of the town. He was aware of the secrets the town kept, and the fear they had of the house. He was aware of everything.

Sadness struck him for a moment, but as often happened, it quickly melted away and mutated into fury. There were times when he felt no humanity at all within himself; there were times when he felt nothing but blind rage, and an unquenchable thirst to inflict terror and misery upon all who dared trifle with him

Bob was also aware of "the plan"—to be carried out by the boy Joey and his friends. He could sense their foolish, childish thoughts on the autumn wind. He would lay them to waste if they dared enter his home again.

The ghost slithered through walls and crawled across the floor. He shook the foundations. He wanted blood.

But first…perhaps a warning…

* * *

Joey could not sleep. His mind would not let him. It was racing with fear, and—he had to admit—excitement. He and his friends were soon going to put Bob Smah's spirit to rest. Not even Chris Lopez could say that!

Outside, the wind was howling like a banshee. Joey pulled his blankets around him and shivered.

Without warning, his television, which rested on top of his bureau, flickered on. Joey blindly tapped around his bed, looking for the remote control he assumed he had accidentally triggered.

Then he found it—or rather, saw it—resting on top of the television.

He froze.

Static was on the television screen before an image flickered to life. It was a logo for Chris Lopez's show, *Spooky Mysteries*. But there was something different about it—though what it was, Joey couldn't be sure. Everything seemed off…slightly askew. Even the image of Chris Lopez that suddenly appeared on the screen—standing in a foggy graveyard—seemed wrong. Joey had just met the man in person, and the image he was seeing on the television was not clicking with his memory.

"Haunted houses are reported all over the world," Chris said on the television, "but none are quite like the infamous house on Creep Street."

Joey shuddered. He had seen every episode of *Spooky Mysteries,* and he knew for a fact this had *never* been a real episode. And yet here it was, on his television. He watched, transfixed.

The image on the television switched to footage of the Smah house. Chris stood on the lawn, still talking directly to the camera.

"We're here, in the quiet town of Blackwood, about to explore the notorious Smah house. Who knows what horrors await within?"

Chris walked through the front door, followed by a crewmember holding a tiny video camera, and the main cameraman filming all the action. The interior of the house was dark, shrouded in shadow. It looked almost a hundred times bigger on this phantom television show than it had in person.

"Let's go upstairs," Chris said. The crewmember with the tiny video camera went first. Suddenly, the stairs began to shake. The crewmember turned to the main camera, a terrified look on his face.

"What's go—" he began, but was cut off in mid-sentence as a rafter swung down from above, smashing into his face. He screamed and fell over the railing, crashing to the floor below.

Chris and the other cameraman began shouting in fear. The camera was shaking, making Joey feel sick to his already lurching stomach. The camera swung up, revealing the floating specter of Bob Smah. His eyes were pitch-black, and he smiled with a mouth full of razor-sharp fangs. The ghost lurched forward, directly at the cameraman, that ghoulish face engulfing the entire screen. The cameraman screamed, and the image on the television shook violently, toppling to the floor. The camera landed on its side, revealing the bloody hand of the cameraman.

Chris crawled out of the darkness, picking the camera up and pointing it directly at his face. He looked terrified, his eyes bulging. "Joey, DON'T come to this house!"

he said directly to the camera. "Whatever you do, STAY OUT of the house on Creep Street!"

Chris' face suddenly morphed into the hideous rictus of Bob Smah. "Or a few nasty *accidents* might happen to *you* and your stupid friends, *too*," he said, and began to laugh maniacally.

The volume on the television grew louder and louder, and Bob's laughter increased. Joey jumped from bed and pressed the OFF button…but the television stayed on! Joey tried the remote, but the laughter continued. He finally dove to the floor and unplugged the television. The image flickered off.

He exhaled and turned back toward his bed…walking right into the thick, bulging chest of Bob Smah, who towered several feet over him. Bob hissed like a cat, his mouth open wide in a terrifying grin.

Joey woke from his nightmare and shot up in bed, almost tumbling to the floor. His heart was pounding and he held his chest with one shaking hand until it finally calmed.

Just a stupid dream.

And it was…but it wasn't. Joey realized this for the first time. He was risking his life—and the lives of his friends—by going back into the house to set Bob Smah's spirit free.

The nightmare may not have been real…but the danger it promised was. Joey realized he couldn't march in there with his friends without some kind of real protection. But where would one find that kind of protection? Something a person could use to fight ghosts?

It was time for another visit to Michael.

CHAPTER FIFTEEN

Halloween had finally arrived in Blackwood, and Joey yearned for the years past when his biggest problem was determining which costume he would wear. Now there were other issues at hand.

School had just ended, and the boys were finalizing their plan of attack. While doing so, they had all learned of Joey's eerie nightmare about Bob Smah.

"Why would I have this nightmare now?" Joey asked. "Why all of sudden?"

"It's because of everything that's been going on," Barry said thoughtfully. "One of us was bound to have nightmares at some point."

"I guess," Joey said, wanting to believe his friend. "But it didn't feel like just any old nightmare. It felt like…a warning."

The three boys continued to walk their bikes to Michael's store. Upon arriving there, Joey tugged open the front door and they entered.

"*Velcome* to my coffin!" said Michael, who suddenly appeared behind his front counter wearing a very cheap vampire cape. The boys turned in alarm and saw Michael, who curled his hands like a vampire and laughed in a terrible Romanian accent.

"Michael, what gives?" Joey demanded, leaning against the counter. "Why did you tell my dad we've been messing around with the Smah house?"

"I'm sorry," Michael said, his voice returning to normal. He lowered his cape-covered arms. "Was I not supposed to?"

"NO!" all three boys shouted at him, and Michael stepped back in surprise, raising his hands in surrender.

"Whoa, sorry!" he said. "But your father and I have been friends ever since we were kids and we threw those moonpies at Sister Tabitha. We tell each other everything!"

"From now on, *anything* we talk to you about remains a secret—got it?" Joey asked.

"I'm not sure I can agree to that, Joey, " Michael said. "It would be irresponsible of me if I knew you were doing something potentially dangerous and I didn't tell your parents."

"Oh, come on," Joey said. "If that's the way you're going to be, then we can't tell you any more secrets."

"Oh, come on!" Michael said, sounding even more childish than Joey. "Include me! I want to be included!"

"You have to swear to secrecy, Michael," Joey warned. "We have to be able to trust you completely. And we can't do that if you run and gossip about us with my parents."

"Fine," Michael agreed, and held up one hand in Scout's Honor.

"Good," Joey said, exhaling in relief. "My dad yelled at me because of your tattling, you know. If you see him, *don't* tell him we're going back to that house tonight. In fact, don't even tell him I was *here* today."

"You're the boss," Michael said. "Apparently. Say, what do you need, anyway? Some werewolf pellets? Perhaps a shrunken head from New Guinea?"

"We don't have time for anything silly," Joey answered. "We need something to ward off ghosts. Got anything like that?" He looked around the store as if he would spot something immediately.

"I sure do," Michael said, grinning. "I have all kinds of stuff: potions, blessed religious relics, texts, t-shirts—"

"We need the most powerful thing you have!" Joey demanded.

"Hmm," Michael said, tapping his index finger against his lips as if he were deep in thought. "I'll be right back." He walked off toward the back of the store, weaving in and out of his few customers and crooked aisles.

"Do you really think Michael has something that could help?" Kevin asked, disbelievingly.

"We've got nothing to lose," Joey reasoned.

"Right," said Barry. "Until we end up waving a plastic toy cross at Bob Smah, who then laughs and punches our heads off."

"That's not funny," Joey said.

"No, it's not," agreed Kevin. "And neither is what we're doing. At this rate, I'd much rather go trick-or-treating than mess around in that old house."

"Too late for that, Mr. Cool," Joey said flatly.

Michael returned with a small wooden container, almost like a jewelry box. It looked hand-carved from dark pine, and strange symbols were etched all around the box itself. He opened the box to reveal a quarter-sized orange diamond, bordered by white gold that was forged in intricate designs. Small wisps of the silver curled along the border like tree branches.

"This," Michael said, "is the Amulet of Demeter. She was known as the goddess of—"

"Harvest!" Barry blurted.

Everyone turned their heads and stared at him.

"What?" he asked, his eyes defensively darting back and forth from Joey and Kevin. "Michael can know that stuff and I can't?"

"He's right," Michael continued. "She was the goddess of harvest. It's claimed that she wore this very amulet around her neck and was the source of all her power."

"What does harvest have to do with anything?" Joey asked Michael, confused.

"Do you know what today is?" Michael asked.

"Halloween," said Kevin, though by his tone, he might as well have said "duh."

When the realization set in, all three boys' eyes went wide. "Halloween!" they all said in unison.

"Halloween," Michael said, agreeing, "the origin of which dates back a time long ago, when people made offerings to the gods and goddesses in exchange for a bountiful harvest."

"And Bob died on Halloween!" Barry said. "If this amulet thing doesn't work, then nothing will!"

Joey went to reach for the amulet, but Michael let the heavy pinewood lid fall, blocking his access.

"Only $29.95, plus tax!"

"MICHAEL!" all the boys shouted, and he laughed in response.

"Guys, this is a business," he said matter-of-factly. "I can't just give this stuff away."

"I don't have that kind of money!" Joey said, his heart sinking. "I just spent most of it on a brand new Big Blood costume!"

"Wow, so how many of those do you have now? Like, five?" Kevin asked dryly.

"Sorry, kids," Michael said. "I need money to keep my store open. And if I were to close tomorrow, who else would give you the supplies you'll need for all your future investigations?"

"What makes you think we'll be making a habit of this?" Barry asked.

"Please," Michael scoffed.

Joey rifled through his pockets and retrieved $8.16. He slapped it on the counter.

Barry also checked his pockets before withdrawing three jellybeans and a quarter. He deposited them sheepishly on the counter. Embarrassed, he shrugged at Joey. "Sorry, I spent all my money on Slushee."

Joey's face fell.

Kevin sighed and took his neon green Velcro wallet out of his pants. He withdrew a twenty-dollar bill and tossed it on the counter.

"That's all my money," Kevin said.

Joey looked at Kevin in awe, resisting the urge to throw his arms around his friend in appreciation, before eagerly turning his attention to Michael. The man considered it a moment, but then nodded.

"Call it a 'friends & family' discount. AND I get to keep the jellybeans." He grinned and handed the box to Joey, who took it gently and opened the lid to see the amulet again.

The carved stone glowed brilliantly, catching the dim lighting of the store and transforming it into a bright, star-shaped hue.

"It'll work," Joey said confidently. "Thanks, Michael."

"Good luck with it, boys," Michael said, and watched the kids leave his store before recording the sale in a thick ledger on his counter.

Outside, the boys gathered around their toppled bikes as Joey slid the box into his sweatshirt's front pocket.

"So, what's next?" Kevin asked, picking up his bike and throwing one leg over the seat.

"Well," Joey began, checking his watch and seeing it was five o'clock, "we gotta make it look like we're going trick-or-treating, so leave your houses wearing costumes. Barry and me will meet you on Creep Street later tonight at seven. It'll be nice and dark by then. No one will see us go in."

"Yeah," Kevin muttered. "Nice and dark."

The three boys rode off together down Main Street toward their homes, weaving in and out of the many trick-or-treaters already staking their candy claims around their small town. Witches and skeletons; princesses and soldiers—they all ran up and down the sidewalks, relishing this one night of the year when they were truly free from parents, teachers, bullies…and their own fears. And they would soon return home with a bag full of their favorite treats and feast on them in front of the many monster movies sure to be playing on television.

Those kids were lucky to enjoy just another normal Halloween.

Other kids weren't so lucky.

Other kids were going to be facing their fears head-on.

Other kids would be lucky to return home at all.

CHAPTER SIXTEEN

Joey looked at his reflection in the bathroom mirror—and a monster looked back at him.

His face was painted a ghostly white and splashed with fake blood. His eyes had dark circles painted under them. He wore all black, with white skeleton gloves, and a rubber knife was tucked into his belt. A beekeeper mask—the most important part of the ensemble—completed the costume. Big Blood lived again, if just for one night.

"Let me see!" he heard Mom say from the hall. Joey stepped out and she snapped a photo of him, blinding him with the flash. "Oh, you look adorable!" she exclaimed.

"He looks stupid," Mario said, though his "costume" merely consisted of a plastic skeleton mask. He and his friends were going to a party, and none of them had put any real effort into their costumes.

"Whatever," Joey said, not feeling up to a battle of idiocy with his brother.

Dad came into the house wiping his hands on his overalls. "Kids are all over the block," he muttered, looking at the mail piled on the table by the front door.

"I know!" Mom said cheerfully. "We've already had several kids! I might have to run out and buy more candy!"

Just like Bob Smah's mom, Joey thought glumly.

"I'm gonna go wash up," Dad said, uninterested.

Mom sighed.

"I'm outta here," Mario said, leaving the house.

"Now, Joey," Mom said. "Remember, if anyone gives you unwrapped candy, throw it in the sewer."

Joey sighed. "Yes, Mom, I know."

"And be careful!"

"I will," Joey said. It suddenly dawned on him what a reverse of the norm Halloween was. In a world growing increasingly more afraid and paranoid, Halloween was an assault on one of the earliest rules your parents ever taught you: don't take candy from strangers.

Halloween had always been a fun night for Joey—a night he looked forward to more than any other night of the year. But this year, he was learning that Halloween was more than a night for taking to the streets and having fun.

Halloween could be dangerous, because some monsters were real.

Mom leaned in and kissed Joey's forehead, smearing some of his make-up. "Have fun!" she said.

Joey nervously smiled and left the house.

The sun was starting to set, casting long shadows along the sidewalk. Costumed children ran up and down the block, their laughter echoing. The air was cool and crisp, and scented with cinnamon. Jack-o-lanterns burned. It was a perfect Halloween for Joey Tonelli.

He wondered if it would be his last.

He rode his bike down the street to Barry's house. Sandra was out on the porch and dressed as a witch—a very pretty witch. Joey couldn't help but stare at her.

"Hi, Sandra," Joey croaked. "Happy Halloween."

"Whatever," she said, yawning.

The front door opened and Barry came out. He had on yellow sweat pants and a yellow sweatshirt with the word "MUSTERD" written on it in black marker.

"Barry, what the heck are you supposed to be?" Joey laughed.

"Mustard!" Barry said proudly, and Joey laughed again.

Sandra rolled her eyes. "You're an idiot," she muttered.

"Bye, Sandra!" Barry said cheerfully. "Have a nice Halloween!"

Sandra did not reply.

As the night approached full dark, the boys rode their bikes to the house on Creep Street, where they both saw Kevin fast approaching from his house on Stine Court. He was dressed as a "baseball player," which really meant he was just wearing his little league uniform.

The three boys came together on the sidewalk and stopped, avoiding looking up at the old house.

"What up, dudes?" Kevin asked.

"Man," Joey started, "you should've seen Barry's sister."

"She is so hot I can barely stand it," Kevin said, his face scrunched as if he were in pain.

"Oh, man, isn't she?" Joey agreed.

"Guys, shut up," Barry said.

"Can you tell her I like her?" Kevin asked.

"Yeah, dream on, Kevin," Joey said.

"I think she'd go for me," Kevin grinned. "I could show her my fastball."

The boys cracked up. The air suddenly felt lighter, and in that moment, all three of them felt genuinely happy—as if they were just three friends on their way to do some trick-or-treating, without a care in the world.

"So, what now?" Barry asked. "Should we go in…?"

The happy mood suddenly vanished.

"Ya know…" Joey said. "If you guys wouldn't mind, let's trick-or-treat a bit, first."

"Yeah?" Barry asked, hopeful.

"Really?" Kevin also asked, cocking an eyebrow. "All this time you've been dying to get us into this house, and now you finally have the chance, and you want to go trick-or-treating first?"

Joey felt the cool autumn breeze on his face and he took it all in. "Can't you feel it?" he asked.

"Feel what?" Barry asked.

"This is it. No matter what happens tonight, this will be the last time we get to do this. I've been trick-or-treating with you guys since forever. Remember when our moms used to push us side by side in strollers on Halloween when we were babies? This is it. You guys were right, we're growing up; we'll be teenagers soon. So let's have one last fling. Let's go out in style."

The boys were silent for a moment.

"Besides," Joey said. "Bob Smah might pull our guts out tonight, so we could at least get some free candy first."

Kevin nodded. "Let's do it," he said.

"Yeah!" Barry cried in triumph.

Joey smiled.

The boys dropped their bikes behind the dead black sycamore tree of the old Smah house and made their way through town—first to Stine Court, where people were known to give away king-size candy bars. They spent the next hour knocking on doors and ringing bells. Candy was given out by the handful and dropped into the boys' pillowcases. As their laughter continued, Joey couldn't help but notice that the majority of the trick-or-treaters out that night were younger than he and his friends.

It's true, he thought, *this is our last year doing this. And maybe that's not such a bad thing – to get older. Some people never get the chance to grow up at all. You can keep Halloween alive in your own ways – and it will always be* yours. *It will always be a night that belongs to you, because you keep it tucked away in your heart.*

"I'm glad we're doing this," Kevin said suddenly. "I'm sorry I was such a jerk about Halloween. I forgot how fun this could be."

"Yeah!" Barry said, already eating some of his candy. "This rocks!"

Joey was silent, but grateful.

The darkness of the night was in full force, and the boys were running out of houses. They found themselves drifting closer and closer back to Creep Street. Before any of them knew it, they stood on the lawn of the Smah house, looking up at its dark form.

Crickets chirped loudly and the dead tree swayed.

"Well," Kevin said. "You guys ready to…bust some ghosts, I guess?"

"Let's do it," Joey said. The boys set their candy sacks down on the lawn beneath the tree next to their bikes.

"I hope our bikes are still here when we come back out," Barry whispered.

"*If* we come out at all," Kevin answered.

* * *

He knew they were coming.

Bob Smah drifted through the dusty, cobweb-caked halls and rooms of his house, and he knew in his heartless chest they were coming.

He wanted to destroy them, the meddling boys. At least, a part of him did—a part of him that was changed—or born—the night he died. It was a cloying, insidious voice in his head, egging him on to do terrible things. It preyed on his sadness; on his galactic loneliness. There were always foolish town children who would dare come to his house—trying to prove how brave they were. And when they did, the voice would come to Bob and tell him to show them what fear was *really* like—and he had always obeyed. Children were sent off shrieking into the night.

But Bob had never encountered kids like these—kids who *kept* coming back; who would not be deterred.

The part of him not filled with hate and rage envied them; envied their bravery. There was even a tiny glimmer buried somewhere deep within him that told him he shouldn't chase them off. That maybe—just maybe—these three boys would understand him. And even…be his friend?

But that evil voice returned, cackling, and he knew it was a foolish thought. Why would anyone want to befriend a creature like himself?

Curse them, the rotten, stinking, spoiled brats of Blackwood.

They were coming to his house tonight, and he would let that voice lead him.

They're bullies, Bob. That's what they are. Three cruel bullies—just like those other three boys who harassed you constantly and made your life unlivable. Boys who thought they could get away with anything…

Oh, he would play a game with these three meddlers. And he would win. He was no longer the sniveling weakling he had been in life. No, now he was full of terrifying power.

He was going to kill them all.

* * *

The boys climbed up onto the porch, paused for a moment, then crossed the threshold into the house.

Barry had brought flashlights for each of them, and they shined the glowing beams through the darkness. Everything inside the house—the sheet-covered furniture, and the fading brown walls, and the décor—appeared the same as it did when Joey had last been inside. He wasn't sure what he had expected to see—perhaps some kind of acknowledgment from the house, or the spirit that dwelled within, that the game was on.

"So, what's the plan?" Kevin asked. "Ya know, the *real* plan? Not just 'find ghost, ask ghost to leave, get screamed at by ghost?' "

Joey grabbed his Big Blood beekeeper mask and pulled it off his head. He dropped it onto the floor next to them. "Chris Lopez told me that if a spirit was sticking around, something might be holding it here," he said. "Like an object."

"Chris Lopez?" Kevin asked. "The *Spooky Mysteries* guy? When did you talk to him?"

"At the mall," Joey said. "I got his autograph."

"Pfft, nerd," Kevin said.

"If we find the object," Joey said, ignoring Kevin, "and bring it to Bob's grave, maybe...I dunno. Maybe Bob will move on."

"That's a big if," Kevin said.

"Got a better idea?" Joey challenged.

"We could go home?" Kevin said, smiling. No one smiled back.

"Let's go," Barry said, moving toward the steps. "If we wanna learn more about Bob Smah, we should probably look in his bedroom."

The boys tentatively climbed the creaking stairs and headed for the door at the end of the hall—the door that had partially hidden the beckoning ghostly figure Joey saw just a few nights ago. The door marked *BOB'S ROOM.*

CHAPTER SEVENTEEN

Joey took a deep breath and opened the door to Bob's room. He stepped back quickly, arms out to shield his friends, as if expecting an instant attack.

Nothing.

Silence.

Darkness.

Joey focused his flashlight's beam on the contents of the room. Seeing nothing, he finally stepped inside, his two friends right behind him.

"Smells in here," Kevin said, and Barry immediately shushed him. "Oh, what, will I offend the ghost?" Kevin shot back.

"Quiet," Joey said, continuing to shine his beam of light across the room.

Kevin grabbed the chain of a small desk lamp, which rested on a table just to the left of the doorway, and yanked it down a few times. The light did not go on.

"Did you really think the electricity still worked in this place?" Barry asked.

"We're investigating a ghost boy, Barry," Kevin countered. "And you're dressed as misspelled mustard. You think trying the lamp is stupid?"

Barry said nothing.

Joey noticed a window in the far corner of the room and crept to it, peering through the dusty and stained glass and down into the street below. "Guys, this is definitely the window—where I saw that face that night. He was staring at us from here."

The bedroom door suddenly slammed shut, rattling many of the framed photos on the wall.

"Jeepers!" Barry yelled and momentarily considered diving under the long-unused bed.

Kevin, catching his breath, slowly walked over to the door, grabbed the knob, and opened it a crack. They all breathed a sigh of relief.

"I expected it to be locked," Joey said. "For good."

Kevin nodded in agreement. He looked out into the hallway, seeing nothing. He softly closed the door again.

"That was just a breeze, right?" Barry asked hopefully. "It was a breeze that slammed the door?"

Joey flashed Barry a quick look that said: *I doubt it.*

Joey's flashlight beam traveled along the framed photos, now crooked from being shaken by the door's violent slam. The circular light helped illuminate some of the wall, but it was still primarily hidden by muddied darkness.

"Guys, shine your light on this wall," Joey ordered, and the boys obeyed. With the help of their lights, he could make out the photos more clearly. There were four of them, and each depicted Bob and his father, Bennington. In one, they were playing baseball, little Bob grinning widely as his father held his arms around him and clutched a bat, showing him the perfect swing; another, sitting around the Christmas tree as Bob opened a train set, which had caused the boy to explode in happiness. But Joey focused on one photo in particular—one where the father and son seemed to be painting stars on a bedroom wall.

Joey took a step back and allowed his light to cascade all around the photos, illuminating the many faded stars adorning the surrounding wall. He looked at the photograph again. Father and son—painting stars for young Bob's bedroom. They were both grinning as they exchanged glances.

The two had shared such happy times, and just like that, his father had been taken. Joey felt a sudden pang of sadness, and he thought of his own father, and how much it would hurt to lose him—especially at Joey's young age.

The last photo appeared to be an official military-issued 8x10 of Bennington Smah in his uniform; an American flag hung in the background.

Joey leaned close and illuminated the nameplate on the bottom of the frame.

Prvt. Bennington Smah, First Class

K.I.A. - December 16, 1944

"That must have been terrible for Bob," Barry began. "To lose his dad when he was…how old was Bob then?"

"Twelve," Kevin answered.

"Gosh," Barry said.

A small table was positioned just below the military photo of Bob's father. On the table sat another American flag, this one folded into a small triangle and placed inside a glass display case. Next to it on the table was another small case, and had an emblem of a gold star flanked by a once-blue ribbon on the top of the lid. The picture was now faded.

"What is that?" Kevin asked.

"It's the Medal of Honor," Barry said. "I think it's the highest honor the military has. That's the medal Mr. Smah got for…" He trailed off, not finishing his thought.

"His family got it," Joey said softly. "Not him. Because he was dead."

"Why would Bob keep this stuff in his room?" Kevin asked. "This photo and this other stuff—it probably reminded him of his father's death every day."

"Not of his death," Joey reasoned, "but of his bravery. Bob probably believed his father was a hero."

Kevin picked up the small case for the Medal of Honor and opened the lid. He held it up to the boys.

"Empty."

Joey suddenly had a flash. The photos in the album Michael had shown them; the later photos of Bob—a medal had been pinned to his shirt in every one.

His father's medal.

A sound from behind them; pained squealing from aging wood. They all turned to see the bedroom door swing open slowly. The boys fearfully gasped at what they saw beyond the doorway.

Nothing.

Nothing at all.

"I can't take much more of this," Barry said, grabbing his chest as if he might have a heart attack any minute.

"Another breeze?" Kevin hopefully asked, the beam of his flashlight shaking across the entrance of the open door.

"Guys," Joey whispered, all of their eyes still on the door. "I think I know what's keeping Bob here."

Silence passed until Kevin looked to Joey. "The medal?" he asked.

"The medal," Joey agreed.

"I hope you're right," Barry said.

"Me, too," Joey said. "But we won't know until we find it. And I think we would find it quicker—"

"Oh, don't even say it," Barry said.

"—if we split up," Joey finished.

"He said it," Barry pained. "He actually said the words 'split up' inside the scariest house on P. Earth."

"We'll be here all night otherwise," Joey said, looking at his friend.

"Let's just do this," Kevin said. "And get it over with. For good."

"Okay," Joey said. "I'll finish up here in Bob's room. Barry, why don't you take the room at the other end of the hallway and work your way down? That way you can check each room. Kevin—"

"Downstairs," Kevin said. "Got it."

The three friends looked at each other—they wondered if for the last time.

"If anyone needs help, just scream," Joey said. "Loud."

Outside, the wind howled and the house's ancient wood creaked.

"That won't be a problem," Barry said.

CHAPTER EIGHTEEN

Kevin was nervous. Anyone in such a creepy house on Halloween night would've been nervous. But he wasn't scared, though—not in the way that Joey and Barry seemed to be. Because unlike them, he was still having a hard time accepting that there actually was a ghost in the house.

Kevin moved about downstairs, billions of dust flecks dancing in the beam of his flashlight.

He checked the living room first. A sheet-covered couch sat in front of a smashed television. An armchair—also covered with a sheet—was to the left.

"So...if I were a Medal of Honor," Kevin began, "where would I hide?"

There was a small table in a corner and he pulled open its drawer, shining his flashlight within. A thick black shadow seemed to be moving against the will of the flashlight's beam. Kevin, confused at first, continued to illuminate the drawer, not exactly sure what he was seeing. And then he realized what it was: hundreds upon hundreds of spiders, their prickly, long-legged bodies scurrying out of the drawer in a hurry. He cried out in shock, staggering backwards and tripping over a footstool.

"Kevin!" Barry called out from upstairs. "Are you okay?"

"Yeah," Kevin called back and sighed. "Just…spiders."

"Yuck," Barry said from above, and then was silent.

"Okay, I should've expected something like that," Kevin said, getting to his feet. "I'm sure at any moment I'm going to open a door and a cat will jump out at me, screaming."

He peeked cautiously into the drawer.

"What the…?" he whispered.

The spiders were gone. He shined his light around the room, expecting to see them on the floor or the walls, or even the ceiling. But they had completely vanished.

That's impossible, he thought. *There were hundreds of them….*

He moved on.

The next room appeared to be some sort of sitting room, or library. There were bookshelves, lined with dusty, rotting hardcovers. A small couch sat by a boarded-up window. He began absently pulling books off the shelf, reasoning that maybe something could be hidden inside or behind them. There were too many books to check, however, and they were all stained and crumbling.

"This is disgusting," he muttered.

He tried one more book called *Heart of Darkness* and saw something small and rectangular on the shelf behind it. Kevin threw the book to the floor and picked up the object.

His eyes went wide.

It was a 1914 Honus Wagner baseball card.

Holy smokes, Kevin thought. *This thing is worth a fortune! And it's in pristine condition!*

He looked around to make sure no one was watching and then tucked the card into his pocket.

"I guess this wasn't such a bad trip after all," he said, smiling.

He moved on to a dining room and didn't see any potential hiding spots—just a table, some chairs, and a broken chandelier overhead. On the wall were three paintings of very stern looking people in drab clothing.

The last room was the kitchen. The tile floor, which had probably once been white, was now moldy and colorless. A fly buzzed by Kevin's ear and he swatted it away.

An old boxy refrigerator had several pieces of paper stuck to it with letter-shaped magnets. Kevin focused on one of the papers and saw it was a math test. At the top of the test was the name Bob Smah, and next to it, an A+.

"Good job, Bob," Kevin muttered. "I've never gotten an A in math class." Another fly buzzed by Kevin's ear, and he swatted it away, too. "Get out of here," he muttered.

He began pulling open drawers, finding utensils and an old cookbook. One drawer was completely filled with long rusty knives.

But no Medal of Honor in sight.

He opened cabinets, seeing several canned goods and an ancient looking box of cereal—nothing of real interest. The only thing left to check was the fridge itself.

"Might as well," he said, shrugging, and pulled open the door. Even though it had been established that there was no electricity in the house, light flooded out of the refrigerator.

Kevin's eyes went wide.

The refrigerator was empty, save for one item sitting on the center shelf: a severed and skinned cow's head on a white plate pooled with blood. Flies darted around it, their buzzing prominent within the cramped refrigerator. Suddenly, the cow's big black eyes began to twitch and roll.

"N-no…" Kevin whimpered. The skinned cow head opened its mouth and began to laugh—a horrible, bloodcurdling laugh. It then began screaming. More flies escaped from its shrieking mouth.

Kevin cried out again and slammed the fridge door shut.

The drawer with the rusty knives suddenly flung open, and all at once, the knives began to hurl themselves out, right at Kevin. He dropped to the floor as they stabbed into the wall above him. Embedded in the hard wood of the wall, the knives wobbled, their handles tapping against each other, the rusty steel of their blades humming with vibration. He jumped to his feet and ran into the dining room, his flashlight beam dancing across the walls. He saw with growing horror that the three paintings had changed; they were no longer of random people. Joey, Barry, and Kevin themselves were now the subjects of the paintings. And in all three, the boys were dressed in black suits and lying in coffins, their hands folded on their chests, their eyes closed.

"Guys!" Kevin screamed. "We gotta get out of here!"

He felt a sharp burning pain in his pocket—the same pocket where he had placed the baseball card. Kevin pulled the card out of his pocket; it was hot to the touch. And it no longer depicted Honus Wagner.

The card now portrayed Bob Smah, dressed in a baseball uniform stained with blood.

"Hi, Kevin!" Bob said from the card.

Kevin screamed. He dropped the card to the floor.

"Welcome to my home!" Bob said from the card. "I hope you like it, because you're gonna be here forever!"

Kevin turned to run. In his terror, he did not see the hole in the floor he was running toward—the hole that had not been there before. He lost his footing and fell, down into the basement, screaming the whole way.

And everything went dark.

CHAPTER NINETEEN

Barry, his heart still pounding, crept toward the closet in the room he was searching.

"You just about scared me half to death, Kevin," he said to himself, his voice still shaky and weak. But he wasn't surprised, either. Kevin, for as fearless as he seemed to be, was terrified of spiders.

I guess we all have that one thing that scares the cream out of us, Barry thought.

He was in the master bedroom. It was larger than Bob's room, though not by much. The furniture was covered in dusty white sheets. Grungy wallpaper peeled off the walls in rips and tears, its color or designs impossible to tell in the darkness.

In the corner of the room sat a freestanding wardrobe cabinet. He crept toward it, half-expecting something to jump out at him in the gloom. His hands slipped around the cold steel knobs of the double-door closet wardrobe, tension creeping up his back.

He was about to yank open the doors of the wardrobe when he heard Kevin call out again—much louder than before when the spiders had given him a good scare. Barry hurtled to the hallway and called out.

"Kevin, are you all right?"

Silence.

"Kevin!" Barry called out again.

When there continued to be no answer, Barry took one step out into the hallway...and Kevin finally responded. "I'm fine, Barry," he said from somewhere down below, his voice oddly cool and collected—especially for someone who had just been screaming his head off. "I'm just fine."

"Are you sure?" Barry cautiously asked.

"Just fine, Barry," said Kevin. "Just fine."

"Did you find anything?" Barry called down.

"Not a thing, Barry," Kevin's unseen voice said back. "Not a thing."

Barry looked down the long hallway to Bob's room, where Joey had remained behind to search. The fact that Joey hadn't even popped his head out in response to Kevin's shouts was at first alarming, but then annoying.

Boy, he gets so obsessed with this stuff that he disappears into his own little world, Barry thought bitterly. *He could at least come out to see if his friend needed help.*

Barry waited a moment longer to listen before turning back to his own searching. He made his way over to the wardrobe again, hesitated, and yanked open the doors. He stifled a scream at the figure that waited for him inside the wardrobe, but then realized the face staring back at him was his own, courtesy of the mirror that lined the entire back of the closet. He sighed heavily in relief and laughed.

C'mon, Barry, he said to himself. *I know you're scared and all, but are you really so terrified of your own reflection, especially when wearing your ridiculous red "KECHUP" costume?*

Barry shook his head again and shut the wardrobe door, turning his attention to another part of the room.

And then his heart stopped, missing several beats, before it kicked back in, working overtime.

KECHUP?

Barry ran back to the wardrobe and pulled it open, again seeing his reflection. Only…it wasn't *his* reflection. Because, while *a* Barry was staring back at him from the mirror, this Barry wasn't frazzled and confused and terrified. No, this Barry—Red Barry—didn't seem scared at all.

"What is this?" Barry called into the mirror, and his non-reflection smiled back.

"What…is…this?" Red Barry repeated, though free of worry, and grinning a wrong looking grin.

"Oh, my god," Barry said, his hand lunging to his mouth.

"Oh…my…god," Red Barry said, his hands slowly creeping to his own mouth. But Red Barry wasn't covering a mouth agape in shock and horror; he was instead covering his ghastly, inhuman smirk—a smirk so far removed from anything resembling warmth or normality that it became sickening. He covered his grinning smile like a person up to unhinged mischief.

Barry's hands dropped heavily from his mouth just then and he felt very heavy on his own two feet. His body wobbled back and forth, threatening to give way and topple at any moment.

Red Barry's own hands lowered slowly from his mouth, revealing his suddenly too-large teeth, now stained with blood.

"Whaddya say, Fatso?" Red Barry said, blood misting from his lips as his words spit red all over Barry's yellow costume—misting impossibly from the other side of the mirror. "Wanna grab a snack?"

Red Barry held up a plate—a sterling silver plate, intricately carved and designed. Resting on top was a pile of squirming worms, all wriggling over each other and falling off the platter and plopping onto Barry's shoes.

Red Barry tossed the platter through the mirror and it bounced off Barry's yellow costume before clattering to the ground.

Barry turned on his heels and lunged down the hallway and into Bob's room, where Joey should have been searching the drawers for signs of the Medal of Honor. It was then that Barry saw why Joey hadn't come out of the room earlier in response to Kevin's panicked cries. It was because

Joey was sitting on the bed and talking to someone next to him—someone a little younger looking; someone seemingly from another time; someone who was impossibly tinted in black-and-white, as if he had just somehow stepped out of an ancient photograph.

It was Bob Smah.

Joey leaned down as Bob held up a hand to shield the words he was whispering into Joey's ear. Joey laughed in response.

Barry's mouth dropped open and for several moments he did not move—could not move. Finally, his eyes shifted over to one of the framed photographs on the wall—to the one that once depicted father and son painting stars on a bedroom wall. Only now it was different. Now, the father was in the picture painting stars by himself, next to a faint outline of an empty void next to him—the place where Bob had once appeared in the photo.

"Joey," Barry whispered, but his friend ignored him, only continuing to laugh softly with Bob.

"Joey!" he called again, louder this time. Both Joey and Bob looked up at Barry. Joey seemed happy to see him, while Bob just looked at him with disinterest.

"Barry!" Joey called merrily—too merrily. "Barry, guess what—this whole thing has been one misunderstanding! We're gonna go now. Bob doesn't need our help!"

"Huh?" Barry asked, shocked. "What is going on?"

"Everything's just fine, now!" Joey said to Barry. "Just fine!"

"What…? But he's…what?" Barry could only say.

"Go on and get Kevin!" Joey continued, a little too loudly now. "He's in the basement! Waiting for you! Go on and get him, and then we can all go home!"

Barry was in complete befuddled shock, and all the while Bob continued to stare disinterestedly at him.

"Joey, seriously, you need to take a second and tell me what's going on!" Barry said, his voice growing panicky and high. "I just saw something really messed up in that other room. Something very weird is going on. I don't think you should trust—"

"Go get Kevin in the basement, Barry," Bob said through an unsettling smirk—a smirk that looked familiar. "He's waiting for you."

Barry, his mouth still agape, raised his heavy head to Joey, who only nodded back in agreement.

"He's waiting for you, Barry," Joey said. "In the basement."

Barry, his mind swimming with a thunderstorm of colliding thoughts, was barely aware that he had slowly turned, walked down the hallway, and plodded down each creaking step of the staircase.

What is going on here? Barry wondered as he searched blindly on the first floor until finding the cellar door. He yanked it open and peered down the dingy steps that stretched off into the unseen dark.

I need to find Kevin. Then we can go ask Joey what exactly is going on, he thought.

He took a breath and began his slow descent down into the darkness of the basement, the door swinging slowly behind him until it shut and locked with a soft click.

CHAPTER TWENTY

Joey carefully dug through the closet in Bob's bedroom. The dead boy's clothes still hung there, and touching them made him feel uneasy. They felt as if they were covered in dirt, and several moths even fluttered from them. Joey looked up and out into the hall. Barry was standing just outside the door and looking at him with a blank expression.

"Find anything?" Joey asked him, turning his attention back to the bottom of Bob's closet. He found a shoebox in the back and slowly pulled it out. The box was filled with random items: green plastic army men; a handful of jacks; a sling-shot; several black-and-white photos of Bob with his parents; a photo of Bob and a dog—a German Shepherd. And at the very bottom, a tiny notebook.

JOURNAL was scrawled across the cover in child-like writing.

Joey's eyes went wide.

"Barrman, check this out!" he said. He flipped open the journal to a random page. There was no date, but the entry read:

"The army sent us Daddy's medal today. Mom said I could wear it, to remember him by. Just looking at it makes me feel like crying sometimes, but it also makes me happy. Dad was real brave. And now I've got this to always remember what a hero he was. I'll never take it off."

Joey couldn't help but feel guilty as he ripped into the Smah family's cursed history, but he knew it was necessary. He flipped to another random page.

This page wasn't dated, either. But as Joey read, the contents made his chest ache ever so slightly:

"The Terrible Trio is after me again. They just won't leave me alone, and I never did nothing to them! The worst is Tough Buggins. Sometimes he gives me this look like he wants to kill me. They jumped me on my way home from school today: Tough, Wendell, and Ralph. I was walking home, minding my own business, and they pulled me into an alleyway and started slapping and punching me with no warning. I begged them to stop, but Tough just laughed and laughed, and Wendell laughed, too. Ralph just stood there, his hands in his pockets. Tough even yelled at Ralph, told him not to stand there like a dope. So Ralph pushed me, hard. I fell into a trashcan and messed up my clothes. I don't get Ralph. He never really hurts me as much as the other two, he usually just sort of stands there. It never

seems like it's his idea to hurt me. I don't even know why he hangs around with those jerks!

"After they were done whooping me, they stuffed me into a trashcan and left me there. Even though I was pretty sure they were gone, I waited, crouched down low for almost an hour, to make sure the coast was clear. By the time I crawled out of the trashcan and got home it was almost dark, and Mom was real sore at me. Yelling and screaming and asking me if I knew what time it was. I just couldn't take it no more. I started crying, and I couldn't stop, and she asked me what was wrong, and I finally told her all about the Trio and how they've been picking on me all this time, and she started crying, too, and said she was so sorry and she hugged me and it was the first time she had hugged me in months, and I felt real happy for once…"

"Poor Bob Smah," Joey said, flipping the pages and not wanting to read anymore. "It was like the kid never had a chance. "

He was about to close the journal when he noticed the next dated page: October 31st, 1945.

The day Bob was murdered.

"Halloween is today. Can't say I'm very excited. I don't have many friends, and it ain't no fun to go out alone. Dad

used to take me out trick-or-treating, and, well…he can't do that no more. I'm also real sad because we had to put Rusty to sleep. He was real sick and real old, and toward the end he was starting to get real mean… but he was still the best dog on earth. I sure do miss him. He was my best – and I guess, only – friend. Now I got no one.

"Mom is doing a lot better than before. She ain't crying as much as she used to, and she's been spending a lot more time with me, but she's so busy with work now, she ain't around that much. I get so lonely sometimes…"

Joey slammed the book shut. He felt pain in his stomach, and he no longer wanted to look at this book. He no longer wanted to be in this house, or in this world, where boys grew so lonely and ended up dead before they had a chance to *finish* growing up.

He flung the book to the back of the closet. He got up and kicked over a trashcan, and then he kicked against a nightstand. He began flinging open drawers and pulling out their contents. He was overcome with anger and sadness, and he wanted to find that lousy medal and end this once and for all.

"Where is it?" he yelled. The house creaked in mocking response.

Joey looked back up to the hallway. Barry was gone.

"Barry?" Joey called out. He stepped from the messy room out into the hall. "Barry, you out here?" He opened a door—saw it was a bathroom. Empty. He tried another door and saw a closet. Also empty. He opened door after door until making it to the last room at the end of the hallway, where Barry had been searching. Joey peered inside from the doorway and guessed it was Bob's parents' room. It was also empty.

"Barry?" Joey called out over the upstairs railing. "Kevin?"

Silence greeted him. Horrible, cold silence.

They left you, he thought suddenly. *You're all alone. Just like Bob Smah. They never wanted to come trick-or-treating with you anyway; you had to practically beg them. They're not your friends. They pity you, Joey. They feel bad for you. They think you're pathetic…*

Joey was becoming increasingly aware that the voice in his head was not his own. No, it sounded like the childish voice of Bob Smah. Joey put his hands over his ears and screamed, "STOP IT!"

Everything was silent again for a moment, and then the voice whispered in his mind:

You're going to die in here…

"Guys, answer me!" Joey called out, and cringed. His voice sounded like he was on the verge of tears. "Tell me where you are!"

There was a sound then—a sound coming from Bob's bedroom. A low, harsh growling sound. Joey slowly turned around. The growling sound increased, and with it came the sound of something clicking against the floorboards.

...we had to put Rusty to sleep. He was real sick and real old, and toward the end he was starting to get real mean...

Joey shined his flashlight. Out of the bedroom shadows came a dog. It vaguely resembled the dog he had seen in the photograph. But this was no natural dog. This thing was twisted and malformed. Its eyes glowed red. The snout was decayed, the flesh and hair gone so that the yellowed sharp fangs were always showing. And there was something all over its fur, especially splashed against its face. Joey knew what it was, of course. It was blood. *Fresh* blood.

The dog barked and snarled. Joey was frozen with fear. He wanted badly to move; his brain was telling his legs to go, but he was stuck fast in place. The dog ran, snarling and snapping its jaws. Joey screamed as it leapt at him, knocking him to the floor. The dog was on his chest now, its hot and putrid breath on his face. It growled and sank its teeth into his neck. The boy screamed, terror racing through his body. He closed his eyes and frantically beat at the dog, still screaming. His hands connected with...nothing.

Joey's eyes flew open. The dog was gone. Joey shot his hands up to his neck, expecting to feel blood. Nothing. He ran to the bathroom and looked at himself in the dirty wall mirror. No marks. He was fine.

Childish laughter filled the house.

"Are you enjoying the games?" the disembodied voice of Bob Smah called out.

"This isn't a game!" Joey yelled.

"Oh, but it is!" said Bob. "I love playing games...because I always win!"

"Where are my friends?" Joey yelled, balling his hands into fists.

"Why don't you check in the basement?" teased the voice. "Why don't you go and see?"

The voice began laughing—an inhuman, cruel laughter that pained Joey's ears.

Joey grabbed his fallen flashlight and marched down the stairs. "I'm not afraid of you!" he called out.

Bob stopped laughing. There was a moment of silence, and then he whispered:

"We'll see about that..."

CHAPTER TWENTY-ONE

"Guys?" Joey called down the looming cellar steps before him. "Are you there?"

Silence.

"Come on, guys, are you down there?" he called again, his voice full of panicky desperation. "Kevin? Barry?"

Again, silence.

"Me and my great ideas," he muttered, holding up his lit flashlight and pointing it down the stairs. With an exhale, he began gingerly stepping down the stairs one at a time. Each step groaned considerably under his weight, and he feared crashing right through them and down to the hard floor below.

It was when he reached the bottom of the steps that the smell of the dank, unlit basement assaulted him. He was as sure as anything that the basement's smell was that of the grave. Cold dirt, soaked with gas and fluid and flesh from a rotting human body—of bones and chemical-soaked cotton. It was a fetid smell and one that knocked Joey back like a punch in the face.

"Ugh," he groaned, his stomach churning and threatening to force its contents out through his curled lips.

A loud CRACK suddenly rang out and Joey instinctually dove to the ground—and a good thing he did. A baseball—which nearly crushed him in the face—bounced off the cold brick wall behind him.

"Foul ball!" called a gleeful voice. Joey managed to hold in his screams of terror, even after looking up into the smiling visage of Bob Smah. It was the face that had haunted him since first seeing it—pale and rotting and sickly.

Grinning and demonic.

Evil.

The face of Bob Smah stared into Joey's own.

Bob wore a baseball uniform—the design of which was seemingly from another era, but was embroidered with a single black skull across the front.

"Man on field!" Bob called to someone behind himself—someone unseen in the darkness.

Joey then saw Kevin standing further in the dark recesses of the cellar, still wearing his baseball uniform. He was robotically alternating between punching his fist into his baseball mitt and adjusting the ball cap resting on his head. He stood on a mound of rich brown dirt.

Kevin was the pitcher.

"Kevin?" Joey asked, and shined the light directly into Kevin's face. His friend only continued to pound his glove and adjust his cap, over and over. Endlessly.

Joey climbed to his feet and began to walk to Kevin when Bob Smah stepped into his path.

"Just in time, Joey!" he called happily. "We need someone to play catcher!" Green-tinted breath leaked from his mouth like a rusty gas pipe, and the stench filled Joey's nose. He ignored his sudden nausea and shined his light into the far corner of the basement where Barry stood, bent at the waist, his hands resting on his knees. He was playing outfield, and in the ready position. An impossible sea of green grass surrounded him.

"Barry!" Joey called to his friend, but like Kevin, Barry did not respond.

"Game on!" called an invisible crowd, and Joey looked sharply to his left and right, shining his flashlight wildly around to locate the phantom audience.

"What is going on?" Joey demanded.

"A baseball game!" Bob called triumphantly, and the unseen crowd cheered.

"What have you done to my friends?" Joey demanded, looking back and forth between Kevin and Barry.

"They joined my team!" Bob happily called. "My baseball team! And now we're playing a game!"

The rogue baseball, previously lost in the dark gloom of the basement, rolled from its corner of blackness and hopped from the floor into Bob's hands. He turned and tossed the baseball to Kevin, who effortlessly caught the ball and immediately pitched it back to Bob.

"Out of the batter's box, Joey!" Bob called and swung the bat with great force. Joey ducked at the last second, feeling the swish of the bat over his head as it connected with the ball.

"Home run!" Bob called. He dropped the wooden bat and vanished into the distant darkness as he ran each base, all while the phantom crowd cheered Bob on and chanted his name. And as he ran, the walls suddenly expanded, as if making room for his victorious tour around the bases.

"Bob! Bob! Bob!" the phantom crowd cheered.

Kevin, all the while, stared back at Joey with his dead dark eyes, unseeing and empty.

"Kevin, wake up!" Joey called. "We gotta get out of here!"

Kevin punched his baseball glove and adjusted his hat, his emotionless eyes seeing nothing at all. The unseen crowd continued its cheer.

"Bob! Bob! Bob!"

"Barry, come on, man!" Joey called into the outfield as Bob rounded second and headed for third.

Barry was motionless, still bent at the waist, still waiting for a fly ball to catch.

"Bob! Bob! Bob!"

Bob rounded third and headed for home, his hat in his hands and waving it at the crowd. He slid home gracefully and then got up, jumping up and down in happiness.

The crowd's chanting of Bob's name then slowly began to drone to a halt, like a tape player with a battery gradually dying. The voices groaned to almost silence, falling several octaves until it sounded like nothing more than a deep, blowing wind.

Bob turned to Joey, burning white fire in his black eyes. "New inning, new position," he said, grabbing at Joey's shirt with his powerful hand. "You're gonna be our catcher. Forever."

"No!" Joey called out and beat at Bob's hand. "We came here to help you!"

"I don't need help!" he growled, his green and foul-smelling breath wafting from his mouth like smoldering candlewicks. "I need a good defense!"

Joey's skull began to tighten and he dropped heavily to his knees as thin bars of metal materialized and began to stretch down his face, one after another, until a catcher's mask had formed. He moaned in pain, ripping at the mask, desperate to remove it.

"I wouldn't take that off if I were you!" Bob said in a singsong voice. "It's dangerous to be on the field without your mask!"

Joey rolled back and forth on the ground in pain as the mask squeezed tighter and tighter around his face. "I…I know what you want!" he managed, screaming in pain between his words. "I know what's keeping you here!"

"Nothing is keeping me here!" Bob said. "Nothing except ME! Because I want to play games! I want to play them forever!" He turned and pointed at Joey's masked face with the baseball bat, which had suddenly appeared back in his hands with a whoosh. "You and your friends—you're going to be my teammates. You wanted in; now you've got in. This was my house, but you three couldn't help but invite yourselves in! So now this is your house, too! For good!"

"We wanted to help you!" Joey managed again, still rocking back and forth from the painful confines of his mask. "We wanted to…find your father's medal!"

Bob's eyes narrowed for a brief second before going wide. His ghostly features—the black eyes and the peeling skin; the foul breath and the insane grin—momentarily vanished. It wasn't Bob Smah, the Ghost at that moment. It was Bob Smah, the Boy.

"Daddy's medal?" he asked, his eyes wide and almost wet, his hands clutching each other in front of his chest like a boy awaiting a prize. "You know where Daddy's medal is?"

The mask around Joey's face ceased its claustrophobic crushing, and Joey immediately ripped it off and threw it aside.

"Joey?" Kevin called from behind Bob, standing no longer on a dirt mound, but simply a hard patch of cold basement floor.

"What's going on?" Barry called from the corner of the basement, the green grass of the outfield now gone.

Joey dared not to answer his friends, but instead continued to look into the childlike face of Bob Smah. "We don't know where it is, yet," he said, choosing his words carefully. "But we can help you find it. We'll find it, and once we do, you can get to see your mother and father again. Wouldn't you like to see them again?"

Bob looked at Joey a moment, his hands still up, his smile warm and genuine. His eyes then rolled over black. His sneer returned and his skin degraded back to slime. "Nice try," he said. "But we're nowhere near nine innings, Joey. Not even close. I'm not going anywhere. And neither are you."

The phantom crowd cheered.

CHAPTER TWENTY-TWO

"Dummy up, everybody!" Joey yelled. Barry and Kevin ran and stood side by side with Joey.

Bob grinned his foul grin and approached them. The baseball uniform he was wearing slowly faded away, and he was now dressed in a striped t-shirt, denim overalls, and sneakers. The boys saw with growing horror that there were rips all over the shirt, and it was stained with blood.

The clothes he was murdered in, Joey thought.

Bob got closer and closer, and the three friends found themselves backed into a corner.

"Joey!" Kevin cried, suddenly remembering something. "The amulet!"

"Holy smokes, I forgot!" Joey yelled. He dug into the pockets of his Big Blood costume and pulled out the amulet Michael had given them earlier in the night. "Get back, you demon!" he yelled, and thrust the amulet into Bob's face.

"Noooo!" Bob hissed. He covered his eyes and moaned as if he had been scalded by flames. "It burns! Oh, it burns!"

"Get back!" Joey yelled, shaking the amulet hard.

Bob continued to scream, but slowly his screams turned into giggles. He looked up, grinning.

"Uh…that's probably not good," Barry whimpered.

Joey looked down at the amulet and turned it upside down. He read aloud the words he saw written there. They were not a magical warding spell, but rather:

"'For use with Pirate Rottenface costume?'"

"Man, Michael totally ripped us off!" Kevin groaned. "Also, we're gonna die!"

"Bob, listen to me!" Joey cried. "I know that the real Bob—the Bob who loved his parents, and who just wanted to grow up and live a normal life—I know he's still somewhere inside, buried beneath this monster! I know you're angry, and you have every right to be! I can't imagine what it's like to be stuck here, all alone—"

Bob laughed. "Who says I'm alone? I have lots of friends! Hundreds! Would you like to meet them?" He grinned wider as a low rumbling sound began. It was followed by a high-pitched squeaking noise.

"What's that?" Kevin asked, shivering.

Out of the darkness of the basement, something was scurrying. For a moment, it looked to Joey that the floor was moving. And then his eyes adjusted and he saw what it really was: Hundreds upon hundreds of fat, gray rats were exploding out through cracks in the floor. They squealed and scampered and clawed at each other.

From more cracks in the walls, spiders began escaping. Large hairy spiders the size of tennis balls, their legs clicking against the stone.

"No!" Kevin whined. "No, no, no!" He broke from his friends and tried to run for the stairs.

"Kevin, no!" Joey yelled, but far too late. A multitude of spiders was upon Kevin, and they began circling him, encasing him in webs.

"Help!" Kevin screamed at the top of his lungs. The spiders worked with preternatural speed, and his entire body was soon covered in white sticky web. He fell to the floor, wriggling in his cocoon. The spiders then wrapped around his face and head, and the boy instantly began struggling to breathe.

"Kevin!" Barry screamed, running to help.

"BARRY, NO!" cried Joey.

The rats were upon Barry now. They scurried up his pant legs, into his yellow mustard costume. He squealed in terror.

"Get them off of me!" he wailed. "Please, no!"

The rats clambered on top of him, weighing him down and sending him hurtling to the floor. They blanketed him completely.

Joey felt like he was going to vomit. He felt his own sanity slipping away; felt his blood go ice cold.

I'm going mad, he thought. *This is what it feels like to go mad…*

His friends, covered in their respective horrors, struggled helplessly on the floor.

Bob grinned, clapping his hands over and over again.

Joey's thoughts suddenly flashed to the dog in the upstairs hall. And to the bizarre baseball game that Bob had made the boys play.

It hadn't been real.

None of it was real.

"Barry! Kevin!" Joey cried out. "It's not real! Don't be afraid of it! It's not real!"

"They can't hear you, Joey!" Bob said. "It's too late!"

"No!" Joey roared. He rushed forward with the useless amulet in his hand. He was sure what he was about to do wasn't going to work—this boy was a ghost, after all. But he was out of options. He smashed the amulet onto Bob's head, and was shocked when it actually connected with something solid, instead of passing right through as he thought it would.

"Ow!" Bob cried in pain and fell onto the floor.

In a wisp of smoke, the spiders and the rats vanished. Barry and Kevin were still writhing on the floor, continuing to fight their invisible adversaries, but they were perfectly fine. This slowly dawned on them, and they looked at each other, confused.

Bob roared. There was a tiny crack in his head where Joey had struck him, and black smoke escaped. "Bullies!" he cried. "Dirty, stinking bullies!"

Joey suddenly remembered the part in Bob's journal about the three kids who used to bully him—the Terrible Trio he had called them. His heart sank into his sneakers.

Oh great, Joey thought. *And there are three of* us, *too…*

"Bob, wait!" Joey said, still trying to reason with the ghost boy. "We're not like those bullies! We're not like the Terrible Trio!"

Bob looked furious. "Yes, you are!" he howled. "You're just as bad as they were!"

He wailed and flew up into the ceiling, disappearing into darkness.

Joey ran to his friends and helped them up. "Are you guys okay?" he asked.

"No!" Kevin shouted. "Can we *please* get out of here?"

"Yeah, Kevin is right," Barry said, out of breath. "It's time to make like a tree and skedaddle!"

"No!" Joey said. "We can't!"

"Why not?" Barry demanded. "Why should we stay here and go through all this?"

"Did you hear what Bob called us before he disappeared?" Joey began, desperately. "He called us bullies."

"So what?" Kevin countered.

"I found a journal earlier when I was searching Bob's bedroom," Joey continued. "Inside it, he talked about these three bullies—he called them the Terrible Trio—that used to make his life miserable. And now look at what's happening to him: three more kids bust in on his house, go through his stuff, bash him on the head? *We* must look like bullies, too. Imagine what he must think!"

"Oh, Joey," Kevin said, without patience. "That little monster has done nothing but mess with our heads and try to scare us half to death ever since we stepped foot in this place. He might even be trying to kill us! Imagine what *he* must think? Who cares what he thinks!"

"Yeah, Joey, forget Bob Smah!" Barry said. "I don't care if he rests in peace or not!"

"Okay, fine. If you won't do it for Bob," Joey said, "then do it for the next person who might come inside this place, not knowing any better. You think we're the first people to ever come in here? You think we'll be the last? And what happens when that *thing* does to them what it did to us? Or worse? Do you want that on your conscience? We're the only ones who can stop him!"

"Let's just call the police!" Kevin said.

"Or our parents!" Barry offered.

"Don't you get it?" Joey said. "No adult will ever believe this. It's only kids like us who will. It's just like those dumb books I read: *The Spook Boys*. Every time they encounter something strange or supernatural, they run to tell an adult, and the adults just laugh at them and think they're nuts. But they're not nuts—they're *always* right. And I know I'm right about *this*. If you guys want to leave, I won't hold it against you. But I'm not leaving until I find that medal, and I set Bob Smah's spirit free."

"If you stay, Joey, you might die," Kevin said. "Do you realize that?"

"I'm willing to risk it," Joey answered. "Don't you see? Bob Smah never had a chance at a childhood. *I* did—we *all* did—and I've spent it whining because...you guys didn't wanna go trick-or-treating? I'm lucky to be alive! Well, until now." He paused a moment. "No. I'm going to set Bob Smah free—whether he makes it easy or not. He's earned the chance to be happy."

The boys were silent for a long time.

"Besides, not to ruin the fabulous time we're all having here, but if Bob doesn't want us to leave...then we're not leaving," Joey offered sullenly.

Kevin and Barry exchanged glances.

"I can't believe I'm even saying this, but...let's do it," Kevin said.

And Barry nodded.

"Really?" Joey asked, surprised.

"We won't leave you, Joey," Kevin said. "We all promised to help you, right? And if we leave you here by yourself, something awful could happen. And *that's* something I don't want on my conscience."

"Yeah, man," Barry said. "We're behind you. No matter what."

"Thanks, guys," Joey said, grateful.

"Now, how do we find that stupid medal?" Kevin asked.

"Michael said Bob died in the basement," Joey said. "And Bob had been wearing that medal in every picture we saw. We checked all over the house and found nothing. It can only be in one place: down here, somewhere."

"Well, let's get cracking," Kevin said. "And Joey…you owe us *big time*."

CHAPTER TWENTY-THREE

Bob screamed, his clenched fists shaking furiously in front of him as he passed through the bowels of his home to a spot he'd discovered long ago—a small closet-sized area of dead space that had somehow been created during the construction of his house. Impossible to reach with a physical form, Bob's spirit had found the room one night as he wept and traveled his dark abandoned house. He'd been alone then. Always alone.

And he was alone now, sinking to the floor of that small, windowless, doorless space. He was fuming, and clawing at his knees, squeezing the denim material of his overalls between his fists. He sobbed loudly, though he lacked the sensation of tears pooling down his cheeks.

Those dirty, rotten, cheating bullies!

Even in death he couldn't escape kids who wanted to pick on him. It wasn't fair!

"What do they want?" he screamed to himself, and pounded the floor a single time. "What do they want with me?"

He raised one hand and held it over the deep, cavernous crack that had appeared in his head when one of the boys, Joey, had struck him. He withdrew his hand and looked at it, but he didn't know what he was expecting to see. Blood? The dark matter that filled his body?

But there was nothing there. At that moment, he would have preferred to see anything at all, no matter how ghastly—bright red blood, a piece of broken skin, a shard of his skull—any sign that he was alive, and that he could feel pain; that he bled and broke like any normal child. But his hand was free of such a sign, and to add insult to injury, he peered effortlessly through his translucent hand and could see the brown floorboards beyond it.

Bob shrieked inside his head as he sat in his hidden room. He pounded the floor beneath him again and again, the sounds emanating around the house like thunder.

How dare they? How dare they come into my house and chase me around just like those other jerks all those years ago?

His eyes rolled over black again, like a great white shark, but his insane grin did not spread across his face. He was so sick and tired of feeling nothing but anger. It was an exhausting emotion to feel day in and day out. And so he let the anger leave his body like a cold wind, and in the wake of its departure his sadness was prominent. But sadness was not the only thing he felt. He also felt pity—for himself, and for the boys he had terrified. They had bullied him, yes, but Bob had bullied *them*, too. And he'd used the power of the evil voice inside him to do it. He supposed *he* was a bully because of that, and that made him feel a little sick in his empty stomach.

It was time for Bob to decide. It was now or never. Would he open the front door and watch them scurry out into the darkness like scared rabbits, leaving him behind forever? Or would he lock the door permanently and prevent them from ever leaving him to the loneliness that had become *his* prison? Would he force them to be his friend—something he'd never really had before?

Bob thought about it for a long time, weighing what he felt was fair and true. These boys had lives to live, much like he had once. They had parents and hobbies and crushes on girls, and all the other things Bob had once possessed in life. Would it be fair to take all of that away from them?

But then he remembered how the Terrible Trio had ruined his already dismal life. How they had antagonized and mocked and struck him when no one was looking. And it all had led to that awful night so many Halloweens ago—when his last breath escaped his small body. It hadn't been fair for Bob then. Should it now be fair for these boys?

He sat there a long time, staring at the dark wooden walls surrounding him. And then he climbed to his feet and allowed his spirit to glide through the floorboards.

His decision had been made.

* * *

Joey tore through the many cabinets bolted high on the basement wall above a dingy washbasin as Kevin searched with his flashlight underneath tables and chairs. Barry had run to the back and was sifting through an ancient furnace with an iron wood-poker, searching the ashes of long-burned coal for signs of the medal.

"It's useless!" Kevin called, slamming the end of his flashlight on the ground. "This thing isn't down here!"

"No, it has to be," Joey said, spinning around to find another place to search. Spying a stack of old boxes in the corner, he ran to them and tore open the cardboard flaps to whip out their contents. More photos, more toys—they rained from the ceiling as Joey tossed them into the air, desperate to find the medal.

A sudden boom rang out, sounding almost like thunder.

"What was that? Is that a storm?" Barry called from the back of the room.

Joey peered out the high basement window into the calm dark night of Halloween. "I don't think so. I think that's—"

Another boom, this one louder, followed by a painful peal of anguished screaming.

"We've gotta find this thing *now,*" Kevin said and got up to join Joey as he searched through the stack of boxes.

"Keep looking through these," Joey ordered, turning to find yet another place to search.

And that was when he spotted it—nestled over in a far corner, not five feet from the bottom of the stairs.

A white door.

"Please be in there," Joey called and ran over to the door. He grabbed the knob and it opened easily with a squeal. Inside was a very small room—a half-bathroom, containing a toilet and a sink. A lone chain connected to a light bulb hung from the ceiling. Disgusting and almost ancient, the small bathroom reminded Joey of jail cells he'd seen on television shows.

Joey cringed at the thought of going anywhere near the dirty toilet in front of him, but he knew it was not the time to be skittish. He ripped open the toilet seat and looked into the rank brown water—an inch or two at most—which remained at the very bottom.

"Ugh," Joey said, his stomach rising again.

"What are you doing?" Kevin asked from behind him, and when he spotted the grungy water within the bowl, he, too, groaned in disgust.

"Bob's mother claimed the plumbing never worked right after Bob's death," Joey said. "Remember Michael telling us that? Maybe the medal is in there."

"All yours, buddy," Kevin said and stepped back.

Joey began to reach his hand into the toilet, his lips stretched thin in disgust, as if preparing to touch something burning hot. Then he stopped. He instead ripped off the lid from the back of the toilet tank. He leaned over it and shined his flashlight. At the bottom of the tank, also pooled with brown water, though less murky, he spotted a small object that had been sucked halfway into a valve. Without hesitating, he stuck his hand into the water, felt around, and pulled out the object:

A very badly worn Medal of Honor, the star rusted and corroded, its bright blue ribbon now rotted to nothing more than a frayed ball of thread.

"Stuck in the valve," Joey said, smiling at the long-lost relic. "Dad, you just saved our lives."

"Did you find it?" Kevin called from behind.

Joey spun around with the medal and held it up. "We gotta get this to Bob's grave, right now!"

"Just in time!" Barry said, looking at his watch. "It's almost midnight!"

"Midnight has nothing to do with anything," Kevin said to Barry, whose cheeks warmed over red.

"Oh."

"Come on, let's get out of here!" Joey said.

They booked it to the stairs and began to climb when Bob materialized at the top in front of the cellar's doorway—their only exit.

"We found your medal, Bob!" Kevin cried. "We found it! If we can get it to your grave, we can set you free! You can be with your parents again!"

Bob was silent at first, and the boys waited for the ghost's response.

"I've been alone for a long time," Bob finally said, sadly. From the dark of the house, and from their distance away from him, it was hard for the boys to judge who was talking to them then—Bob the Ghost, or Bob the Boy. "So very alone," he continued. "Can you picture it? Being alone for as long as I have? For decades? Wandering around this house, and no one to play with?" He raised his hand to the cellar door. "I don't care anymore if you guys wanted to bully me. We can just forget it ever happened. I guess we can't be friends for now, but after a while, we will be. Once you guys understand why I can't let you leave this house. Ever."

He slammed the door and the boys could hear it being locked.

"I won't be alone anymore," Bob said, his voice sounding muffled through the door. "I refuse."

CHAPTER TWENTY-FOUR

Joey ran up the stairs and began pounding on the door, but it wouldn't budge. "Bob, no!" he cried. "We have the medal! Your father's medal!"

"We're doomed!" cried Barry, sitting down at the bottom of the stairs, his back against the wall.

"Face it, Joey," Kevin said as his friend continued to beat on the door. "That thing isn't Bob Smah anymore. Whoever Bob Smah was died a long time ago. That's just some…monster. He doesn't care about his father's medal. He doesn't care about anything, except making other people suffer."

Joey sighed, resting his head against the door. "We were so close."

"So, what do we do now?" Barry asked in an angry voice. "Wait to die?"

"Someone will find us," Joey said. "Someone will figure out we're here." His eyes lit up. "Michael! Michael knows we're here!"

"We told him not to tell anyone, though," Kevin said.

Joey's face fell. "Yeah, but, when we've been missing for a while, he'll know he has to tell someone."

"We might be dead by then," Barry said softly. "Or worse…"

Joey punched the door. Hard. In his grade-school mind, for a brief moment, he actually expected it to shatter against his punch. Instead, it just rumbled on its hinges and sent a sharp stab of pain through his hand.

"If only we had something heavy to break the door down," Kevin sighed.

There was a moment of silence, and then Barry lifted his head. "I'm something heavy," he said.

Kevin and Joey looked at him, puzzled.

"What?" Joey asked, confused.

"Me," Barry said. "*I'm* something heavy." He jumped to his feet. "I'm going to try and break down the door."

"No way, Barrman," Joey said. "You'll bust your head or something."

"Joey's right, man," Kevin said. "You could get hurt."

"It's worth a try," Barry reasoned. "I either try, or we wait down here for Bob to kill us."

Joey and Kevin looked at each other.

"Only one condition," Barry said.

"Name it," said Joey.

"If I do this, you have to promise: no more fat jokes."

"No way, forget it!" Kevin said.

"SHUT UP, Kevin!" Joey said and then looked at Barry. "Of course we promise, man."

"Fine," Kevin sighed, almost sadly. "No more fat jokes..."

Barry, despite being locked within the cellar of a haunted house, facing certain death, looked nearly relieved. Both Joey and Kevin noticed this look fall across their friend's face, and each of them felt instantly guilty.

"Hey, Barrman," Kevin began softly. "When we make those jokes, we're not…trying to be mean or anything. You know that, right?"

"I know," Barry said, nodding. "I know you guys are just fooling around. But it still hurts. Honestly, I've wanted to say something about it for a long time, but I was afraid."

"Of what?" Joey asked.

"That you guys wouldn't want to be my friend anymore."

Joey felt incredibly ashamed. He thought back to Bob Smah's journal—his descriptions of being bullied, and how that must have played a big part in turning him into the ghostly monster he now was. And then Joey thought of all the times he and Kevin had picked on Barry for his weight; Barry, who was probably the sweetest, nicest kid Joey knew. He didn't deserve that.

No one did.

"Sorry, Barry," Joey said. "And I'm not saying that so you'll try to break down the door. I'm saying it because you're my friend, and I mean it. I really am sorry if the things we said ever hurt you."

"Yeah," Kevin said, rubbing the back of his head. "Me too."

Barry smiled sheepishly. "Well…once we're not being almost murdered by ghosts, maybe you guys can make it up to me. But, for now…"

He took a deep breath.

"Clear the way!"

Joey and Kevin stepped back as Barry went to the very back of the cellar, lined himself up with the cellar stairs, and began to run as fast as he could. He hopped steps two at a time, feeling a speed he never thought himself capable of ever achieving. But halfway up the rickety stairs, it dawned on him that this might not work, and he might end up breaking every bone in his body.

Too late now, he thought.

"Ahhh!" came Barry's war cry, and he braced his arms against his face. He made it up the rest of the steps with impressive speed and slammed into the door with a furious power. The door shattered; it broke from its hinges and snapped in half. Barry fell forward with the door, collapsing on top of the rubble.

"Way to go, Fat Man!" Kevin cried, pumping his fists.

"Oh, come on, Kevin!" Joey yelled, slapping Kevin on the back of the head.

"Oh, right, sorry!" Kevin said, sounding genuinely apologetic. "Sorry, Barry!"

Joey and Kevin ran eagerly up the cellar steps and helped Barry to his feet. He shook himself off, dust falling out of his hair.

"Sorry, Barry, really," Kevin said. "It's a habit I'm going to have to break..."

"No problem," he said, smiling. Then he lost his balance and almost fell down. The boys helped up him again. Barry looked at the wreckage of the door. "See, sometimes it pays to have a little extra weight..."

"C'mon, we gotta get to the cemetery," Joey said. "Let's get the bikes!"

The friends moved as quickly as they could through the house and to the front door.

* * *

Bob was in the attic of his house, floating amongst the remnants of his family, and trying as hard as he could to remember what life had been like before...this. But his dead mind wouldn't let him. It knew only pain. And rage, which he tried his best to keep at bay. It knew only misery.

But now that he had these three boys—whom he hoped would one day accept him as a friend—maybe things could be different for him. Maybe he wouldn't be so angry and sad all the time.

And then he heard the sound of the shattering door, followed by running footsteps.

"NO!" Bob screamed. He pulled the boards from the oval attic window and looked out. He saw the three boys jump on their bikes and begin to pedal down the street.

The anger rushed back into him like a drop of blood in water, and his eyes rolled over black again. The sadness and misery were gone. There was now nothing left in him but fury. Bob screamed in rage at their escape.

He wanted so badly to go after them—to kill them all…but he could not. The house had been his prison for longer than he ever dared remember. And it would continue to be so until…who knows? Perhaps when the old wood of the house finally gave in and collapsed in a dusty pile. Maybe then he would somehow be free.

He hadn't left the house since his death. He'd never had a reason to. The years his mother was still alive, he desperately tried to communicate with her; he rattled the doors and moved the furniture and smashed glass. Sometimes he shrieked right in her ears. But she never noticed—or pretended not to. And that was the most frustrating part. Had she actually seen and heard him all that time? Or was it only after her death when he had learned to reveal himself to the living?

He didn't know, and it had only added to his pain.

Once his mother had finally died, he was truly alone, and he had nowhere to go. This house was the only place he belonged. He'd never tried to leave. But now, he badly needed to leave—to destroy the boys who dared enter his home.

Could he even leave? He wasn't sure. But it couldn't hurt to try...

Bob hesitantly stuck his hand through the window, expecting some invisible force field to stop him, or maybe an unnatural burning warning him he was not welcome in the land of the living. Instead, his hand slipped out into the night. His empty eye sockets went wide. He stuck his head out next and felt the autumn air. He began to laugh insanely. He jumped from the attic window and floated gently down to the lawn.

He did not know why he had been granted this reprieve from his prison. Perhaps it was because of Halloween night, and all the legends and lore that went with it…or perhaps it was simply because he had never even tried. But none of that mattered now.

He was out of the house now, and his laughter echoed down the block.

Bob Smah would kill the boys once and for all.

* * *

The friends hopped onto their bikes outside, still by the tree, and pedaled faster than they had ever pedaled in their lives.

"Hurry, it's nearly midnight!" Barry cried.

"Will you stop pointing that out?" Kevin yelled. "There is nothing about this that involves midnight!"

"Sorry!" Barry said. "That's usually what it's like in horror movies!"

"Well, this isn't a horror movie!" Joey said.

Just then, they heard a wild shriek. The boys looked over their shoulders.

The ghost of Bob Smah, it seemed, was no longer a prisoner of his house. He was right behind them, high in the air above, his ghastly grin illuminated by the glow of the moon.

CHAPTER TWENTY-FIVE

The ghost of Bob Smah grinned with pride—pride that he had escaped his house and was now intent on doing just one more thing. Joey did not even want to imagine what that *thing* was…

With the Medal of Honor clenched tightly in Joey's hand, the boys continued to pedal hard down to the end of Creep Street. They fought to ride as fast as they could, and all the while they could hear Bob's ghastly laughter just behind them.

"This is getting ridiculous!" Kevin said and began pedaling harder.

Bob laughed at them again from above, and with each passing house, the unearthly breeze from his near-invisible body extinguished the flame in each of its jack-o-lanterns.

"Guys, come on, get close!" Joey said. Kevin pulled up to the right side of Joey and Barry to Joey's left. "We'll never outrun him and make it to the cemetery in time!"

"You're going to say that stupid thing again, aren't you?" Barry asked. "That stupid thing you said earlier, which got us into a whole mess of trouble?"

Joey nodded. "We have no other choice! We have to—"

"Split up again," Kevin finished, annoyed. "Joey, after tonight, you're never making the plans again. Ever."

"We have to find a way to hide which of us has the medal!" Barry said. "Or we'll never make it to the cemetery alive!"

"Here's what we'll do!" Joey said, and he whispered his plan to his friends.

From up above, Bob glowered down at the boys—especially Joey—and imagined killing them slowly. How he would enjoy that—to stop the breath of the boys who had entered his house, stolen his medal, and dared to think they could vanquish Bob from this earth.

He then saw Joey turn his head, glance at Bob once, and hand off something to Barry.

The medal, Bob thought. *But why give it to the slowest kid there?*

And then Bob saw Joey hand something to Kevin, too.

Bob almost grinned at the sight.

That's pretty smart, Joey, Bob thought. *But are you smarter than me? We'll see.*

Creep Street ended at the next intersection and the three boys suddenly split up, with Barry making a left onto King Street as Joey and Kevin continued across the intersection, where Creep Street became Carpenter Avenue.

Bob considered his options, first setting his sights on Barry, who was heading in the direction of the cemetery. But then Bob stopped—mid-air—and frustratingly watched the other two boys continue to pedal down Carpenter Avenue…away from the cemetery.

"No!" Bob shrieked in the air, kicking in anger. "Who has my medal?" His loud voice shook the small neighborhood. Wild winds followed his angry bellow, violently blowing trees. Halloween decorations swung dangerously back and forth, pivoting around the lone nail that held them in place on their doors and windows.

Joey and Kevin continued up Carpenter Avenue and soon approached another intersection.

"OK, this is it," Joey said, and Kevin stuck out his fist. Joey gave him a pound and nodded at his friend.

"See you soon…I hope," said Kevin, and he made a sudden left turn down Raven Terrace.

Joey took a breath—solo again, for the second time that night—and continued his ride down Carpenter Avenue.

* * *

The tires of Barry's bike screeched as he made the turn onto Main Street, clenching his fist in such a way that he hoped Bob wouldn't be able to tell what was in there. The journey so far had been arduous, and it was catching up with him. His lungs ached and his legs burned as if on fire, but he would not stop.

Joey and Kevin were counting on him.

Bob still loomed above Barry, cackling, and flying lower and lower until Barry could feel the cold of Bob's body just behind him. He resisted the urge to look and instead pedaled even harder, desperate to make it to the cemetery.

And there it was, just up ahead!

Barry exhaled a sharp breath as he prepared for the first part of the plan. His tires skidded just outside the front gates of the cemetery—which were closed and locked tight—and he hopped off the bike and began banging on the heavy bars. He shouted into the darkness beyond them, hoping the old caretaker inside had heard his cries.

Bob landed on the ground directly behind Barry, continuing to laugh. "You should know better than to try and outrun a ghost," he said.

As he advanced on Barry, and his face broke out in another menacing grin, the wind picked up, and the only sound that could be heard was billowing trees, bending so dangerously from the powerful wind that they nearly snapped in half.

* * *

Kevin ducked his head and forced himself through the sudden wind. He wondered if Barry had made it to the cemetery, and if so, how far behind him the ghost of Bob Smah was. He hoped this plan of getting the medal to Bob's grave worked the way Joey promised it would. Because if it didn't, not only would it mean that all the horrors the boys had faced that night would have been for nothing, but it could very well mean the end of their lives.

Kevin bitterly fought such a thought and instead continued to pedal. Thankfully the hour was late, and the streets deserted, or Kevin would have doubtlessly spilled over the hood of someone's car on what was normally a very busy road. He looked all around him to see if he would spot Bob advancing maniacally toward him, but there was nothing but the dark sky and the harsh wind.

Kevin's turn arrived and he cut yet another hard left, down a small alley that led back to Main Street.

And so continued his not-so-direct route to Resurrection Cemetery—to the back entrance.

* * *

Joey's face make-up, filthy and splotchy from the crazy night, caused his skin to itch, but he ignored the sensation. The last thing he needed was to lose control of his bike and end up skidding face-first down Carpenter Avenue.

He took a single breath, preparing himself for the horrors potentially behind him. He hesitated a moment longer, and then looked.

Nothing.

Joey back-pedaled suddenly, applying a quick break to his back tires, and the bike skidded into a semi-circle.

This is it, Joey thought. *I hope this worked.*

He then began pedaling *back* down Carpenter Avenue, opposite the way he had just ridden, hoping Bob had taken Barry's bait.

It was all he could hope for as he continued his journey to Resurrection Cemetery.

The wind suddenly blew hard again, pushing against him, as if daring him to go further. He fought against it and continued his route to the cemetery, hoping and praying that he wasn't too late.

CHAPTER TWENTY-SIX

It has been said that in moments of extreme duress, people can suddenly summon incredible strength—adrenaline kicks in and results in almost superhuman powers.

Nothing could probably be more distressing than being chased by a killer ghost, and so Barry—without even realizing what he was doing—suddenly found himself scrambling up the cemetery gates. His heavy frame did not stop him; he easily climbed and vaulted the gate with a grace he had never before known, thudding on the slightly wet grass on the other side.

And then he was running again, huffing and puffing.

Bob had no need to climb the gate; he merely passed through it, as if it weren't there at all.

Thunder cracked in the sky and lightning ripped a hole in the night. Barry looked over his shoulder and saw Bob slowly stalking after him, like a horror film killer.

The wind howled and gave way to more lightning and thunder; a huge rumble, as if the very earth were being torn apart.

Barry continued to run. It was dark in the cemetery, and he realized he could not remember where the Smah graves were located. He looked over his shoulder again, expecting to see Bob still coming after him. But there was no one. Lightning flashed silently, illuminating the entire cemetery. It appeared empty.

Barry turned back around and screamed. Bob was directly in front of him.

"Hiya, Barry!" Bob giggled. "Wanna play?"

Tripping over his own feet, Barry fell back hard onto the grass, the wind knocked out of him.

Bob loomed above, his terrifying empty eye sockets ablaze. He pointed at Barry. "Give me the medal!" he screamed. "Give me my father's medal!"

Barry shivered. He slowly opened his clenched hand and revealed…a piece of Halloween candy.

"NO!" Bob cried. "*Bullies!* You're *all* bullies! I'm going to tear you apart!"

Bob's face changed; it became even more horrible—the face of some hellish demon. His ears became elongated, pointed like the ears of a bat. Fire burned in his black eye sockets. His nose twisted and split open; worms and tiny insects scurried out. His teeth became gnarled fangs.

"Hey, Bob!" cried a voice. Bob spun around, stunned.

Kevin was there, standing by a tall angel statue.

"GAME OVER!" he cried, and heaved his body into the massive stone structure. It toppled over and crashed onto Bob, flattening him to the ground. The large stone covered him completely, and there was nothing but silence.

"Barry, did you see how awesome I just was?" Kevin cried, excited.

"Help me up!" Barry said, slowly catching his breath.

"Man, I totally saved your bacon," Kevin said.

Barry was about to reply with his thanks, but instead said, "Kevin! He's gone!"

Kevin looked down and saw that Bob was no longer crushed beneath the statue.

"Uh-oh," the boys said in unison.

Another flash of lightning, and Bob was suddenly in front of them. He grabbed them both by their necks and lifted them off the ground, his strength not at all the strength of a human boy.

Barry and Kevin gasped for air, their sneakers dangling a few inches above the ground.

"WHERE'S MY MEDAL?" Bob screamed.

"I don't have it!" Kevin croaked. "I swear!"

"That means your other friend has it!" Bob snarled. "Where is he?"

"Gone!" Barry said, gagging. "A million miles from here! You'll never see him again!"

Just then, Joey's voice echoed across the cemetery. "Guys? Where are you?"

Barry closed his eyes, defeated.

Bob grinned.

* * *

Joey moved through the cemetery, his eyes scanning the graves. The Medal of Honor was tucked safely in his pocket. Now he just needed to find Barry and Kevin—and the grave.

In the darkness, his pocket caught on the branch of a bush and his pants became snagged. He pulled hard on them, startled, and wrenched them free.

"Guys? Where are you?" Joey yelled again. More thunder answered him, and it was beginning to rain. He felt his already messy Halloween make-up running down his face in streaks. He hoped his friends were okay. But the cemetery seemed deserted. From where he stood, he had a pretty good view of the grounds—and he was quite sure there was no one else there. Had they not gotten there yet?

Or worse—had Bob gotten to them first?

"Guys! Tell me where you are!" Joey cried.

"Up here!" called a giggling voice from above.

Joey looked up and gasped.

Bob floated thirty feet in the air. Both Kevin and Barry hung upside-down, Bob clenching both of them by their ankles. Both of the boys struggled, but Bob had a tight grip on them.

"Let them go!" Joey yelled.

"Oh, I'll let them go," Bob laughed. "If you don't put down my medal, I'll let them BOTH go—head first into the ground! SPLAT!" He burst into wild giggles as more thunder boomed.

"Don't do it, Joey!" Barry cried.

"No, you should probably do it!" Kevin said, terrified.

Bob let both of them go.

"NO!" Joey screamed.

The boys fell a few feet before Bob caught them again, giggling more.

"Don't test my patience, Joey," Bob said. "Next time, I might not catch them!"

Joey dug into his pocket, reaching for the medal—and found only a hole.

CHAPTER TWENTY-SEVEN

"I don't have it!" Joey shrieked, and in response, Bob dropped Barry and Kevin again, and they plummeted headfirst over an arsenal of jagged marble tombstones.

"Stop, please!" Joey called, and again, they froze in mid-air.

Barry, upside down, but now eye-level with Joey, looked at him. "Joey, please, just give him the stupid medal."

"I really don't have it, Barry!" Joey said, and looked up with desperation into Bob's eyes. "Honest! There's a hole in my pocket—I must've caught it on something earlier! The medal's gone!"

Bob snarled, but Joey looked to him, hoping for any sign of sympathy.

"Please!"

"Joey," said Bob, speaking to him as if he were a pesky child. "You're grounded."

He prepared to drop Barry again, whose head still hovered five feet over a cross-shaped tombstone.

And at that moment, the events unfolding before Joey Tonelli seemed to grind to a halt, as if everything around him seemed to be happening in slow motion.

The events of the night flashed through Joey's mind: the horrors the friends had faced, the danger they willingly put themselves in—all for the sake of trying to help a ghost who wanted nothing more than to destroy them. Maybe Kevin and Barry had been right.

Forget Bob Smah.

Seeing his friends hanging upside down from Bob's ghostly grip—that was it. That was the last straw.

Joey's angry voice echoed inside his head. *Enough is enough. I've had it with this whole thing—with this malicious ghost and his crappy house and this crappy Halloween. With growing up and facing fears head on. I've had it. With everything.*

"It's true, Smah," Joey said, his voice stronger now—filled with anger and defiance. "The medal is gone. I'm not pulling a fast one. Because let's face it—if I was, you'd kill us anyway. Easily."

Bob grinned and nodded. "I would."

"Uh, Joey?" asked Kevin, but Joey continued his rant.

"The medal is just gone. Because it's a game, Bob. It's called find the medal."

"No more games," Bob said, snarling again like an animal.

"There's always time for games, isn't there, Bob? Isn't that what all of this is?" Joey asked, spreading his arms. "Chasing us around? Making us see things that aren't there? Trying to scare us to death?"

Bob grinned his terrible grin and continued to stare hard at Joey, but he could see that the specter was considering his words. "You're the most fun game I've ever played," he said, his lips curled in a fearsome smirk. "You were so easy—from the start. It's been a blast—it truly has."

Joey said nothing.

"But now you die," Bob continued. "Each of you. Who's first?"

"No, Bob," Joey said. "Not yet. Here's the deal: we each try to find the medal first. Us versus you. If we find the medal, you let us leave. And if you find the medal...well...we'll surrender to you."

Bob, still grasping both Barry and Kevin, zoomed into the air, higher than thirty feet this time. He guffawed. "This could be a trick. You could know where the medal is right now."

Joey shook his head. "I don't know where the medal is. And if I did, you could crawl right inside my head and see if I was lying, couldn't you? After all, isn't that how you knew Kevin was afraid of spiders? And Barry was afraid of rats? And me of..." Joey paused a moment. "...Of being alone?"

Bob grinned and nodded. He was unable to resist this newest "game"—too eager to pass up the opportunity to scare the boys even more. "If I find the medal first…what do I win?"

"Whoever finds the medal," Joey began, "chooses the fate of the loser."

Bob grinned even wider. He let go of Barry and Kevin, but their heavy plummet stopped short, and both boys froze in mid-air just mere feet above the awaiting army of carved gray stones below. They even slightly spun from their suspended animation.

Bob tapped his lips a moment in consideration. And then: "Game on!"

Barry and Kevin floated several feet away from the tombstones until they were over open grass, and then completed their fall.

"Oomph!" Barry said, landing on his stomach.

Kevin was momentarily dazed. "Nice plan," he said, his head woozy.

"Joey!" Barry said. "Did you really lose the medal?"

"I'm afraid so, dude," Joey said, his eyes still warily on Bob.

"How long do we have to search?" Bob asked, his eyes gleaming with eagerness to begin the game.

Joey checked his watch. "It's ten minutes to midnight," he said. "Ten minutes to find the medal and win the game."

Bob narrowed his eyes, but then grinned, nodded, and instantly dissipated.

"See?" Barry gloated at Kevin. "Midnight. Told you it was important."

"Do you have any idea where you lost the medal?" asked Kevin.

"Forget the medal," Joey said dismissively, and Kevin and Barry's mouths dropped open in shock.

"What?" Barry shouted, and even grabbed at Joey's skeleton-frame t-shirt. "What do you mean 'forget the medal'? That's the WHOLE GAME."

Joey shook his head. "Come on, we gotta get to Bob's grave before he finds the medal. I'll explain on the way."

"No, you'll explain *now*," Kevin ordered.

"This is not about some stupid medal," Joey explained. "Because really—what is it? It's a hunk of brass, or whatever. Sure, in life, it represented something really important to Bob. But now? Is that *really* the thing keeping his spirit here?"

"What do you mean?" Kevin asked. "You're not making any sense, and the clock is ticking, man."

"I think the answer is simpler than crawling around these bushes and looking for that medal," Joey continued.

"Bob doesn't need the medal. He needs to finally understand that the only thing keeping him here is *himself*."

"No," Kevin firmly said. "No, this whole entire thing has been about the medal—about getting the medal to Bob's grave. And if you don't want to help us search for it, then don't. But *I'm* going to."

"It's not that I won't help you," Joey reasoned. "It's just that we don't *need* it."

"Well, what can it hurt?" asked Barry. "We find the medal, or we don't find the medal. Either way, I mean…right?"

"Yeah, besides," Kevin continued. "You challenged Bob to find it. It doesn't matter if the medal can defeat him. The game is to find it."

"This whole *thing* has been a game," Joey said. "He's been messing with us. He could've killed us this whole time. And why hasn't he?"

Silence from his friends.

"Because he won't," Joey continued. "Or he can't. His life was taken from him at a young age, and he knows what it's done to him. But inside he's still just a child. And that part of him—the part that's still innocent—won't hurt another human being."

More silence for a moment, no one wanting to make the first move

"There's no time for this," Joey said. "If you want to look for the medal, fine. But I'm going to his grave, and I'll wait for him there."

And with that, Joey took off for the Smah plot, leaving Kevin and Barry to watch him go.

* * *

The ghost of Bob Smah whispered through the cemetery, his eyes scanning the dark grounds below for the medal. His grin intensified as he remembered the rules of their game, and he could not wait to plan the boys' demise—one piece of flesh at a time. It was going to be glorious—the most thrilling game he'd ever played.

"Hee hee hee!" laughed Bob, in pure giddiness. This Halloween night was going to be a massacre.

Something caught his eye and he dove for a closer look. Yes, he could see it—plain as day: a single footprint in the wet, muddy ground. And then another, and another. Rushed footprints, made by someone desperate and hurrying—someone confused. They seemed directionless, but he followed them, anyway. And after each footprint, he scanned the ground for the object—the treasured medal from his past.

And there it was!

Bob roared with glee and snatched the medal into his ghostly hand: the long-lost relic, now finally in his possession after all this time. He rubbed his thumb around the star, long worn down by its watery prison. Though he felt a momentary feeling of victory and vicious pride, the rotten blue ribbon suddenly stabbed him in the place where his heart had once been. He flinched from the feeling, and soon the pain became so unbearable he tumbled to the ground. His black eyes rolled over to reveal normal, childlike eyes, and they soon filled with tears. He remembered the day when the medal came, delivered by a nameless soldier in uniform.

"Here, Bob," Mrs. Smah had said and handed the medal to her son. *"Your father was so brave – the bravest man I've ever known. And he would've wanted you to have this. He would've wanted you to be brave, too. So take it. Take it and remember your father and his bravery. And always be the good person he would've wanted you to be."*

"No!" Bob called once in his boyish voice. He clenched the medal tightly in his hand as the tears spilled down from his angelic eyes. For a moment, Bob wanted nothing more than to be with his family again. To be away from all this death.

The moment, however, was fleeting.

For soon, those angelic eyes vanished, and they filled again with blackness, like storm clouds rolling across a peaceful sky.

"No," he said again, with furious anger. Still gripping the medal, he floated several feet off the ground. He shot like a bolt of lighting into the night sky to locate his opponents.

For what would be their final game.

CHAPTER TWENTY-EIGHT

"I'm going to kill that boy."

Thunder crashed again, and lightning lit up the night in such a way that the outlines of all the clouds became visible for a split second, as if someone had taken an x-ray of the sky. Rain had been falling off and on.

"Give Joey a break," Michael said, smiling. "He's probably still trick-or-treating."

"This late?" Dad demanded.

At Joey's house, Dad and Michael sat on the porch, drinking beer and remaining mostly silent. Dad checked his pocket watch. Two minutes to midnight, and Joey still wasn't home. Mario—who usually stayed out the latest—had been home for hours.

Michael shrugged. "It's Halloween. Kids love Halloween."

"I never loved Halloween," Dad muttered.

Michael laughed. "That's true. I always had to drag you out."

"Where *is* he?" Dad asked, frowning.

Michael took a sip of beer and remained silent.

"He's gonna get it when he comes home," Dad muttered. "I'm going to ground him until he's ready for college. And I swear, if I find out he went back to that house…"

"C'mon," Michael said, grinning. "You know how kids get about that place—the spooky old Smah house. When we were kids, and Mrs. Smah was still living there—all crazy and reclusive—we used to go there all the time. Remember? You and me. We used to peek in through the windows."

Dad smiled slightly. "Yeah. You were obsessed with that place. Kept telling me you thought it was haunted."

Michael chuckled softly. "You know the saying: 'Boys will be boys.' Give Joey a break. Believe it or not—and sometimes I don't believe it myself—we were boys once. And we did stupid things."

Dad sighed and looked down at his work boots. "I guess you're right. I just wish he would get home. It's late, and this storm is getting worse."

"Don't worry," Michael said reassuringly. "I'm sure wherever Joey is, he's safe."

* * *

I'm going to die, Joey thought as he stood by the grave of Bob Smah. *Kevin is probably right – that medal* is *important, and Bob is going to show up and make all my guts fall out through my mouth, like in that movie* The Melting Dead.

Joey rolled up his sleeve and checked his watch. It was two minutes to midnight. He groaned and waited.

* * *

Barry and Kevin were frantically searching the graveyard for the Medal of Honor.

"Found it!" Barry cried out suddenly.

"Really?" cried Kevin, looking up.

"Never mind. Bottle cap."

"You know what, Barry, that's the fifth time you screamed 'found it' and all you had was a bottle cap. Pay attention."

"Sorry. Hey, Kevin?" Barry asked, combing through the wet grass.

"Yeah?"

"What if Joey is right? What if we *don't* need the medal?"

"Does it even matter at this point?" Kevin sighed. "We're toast."

"You got that right," said a voice. Barry and Kevin looked up and screamed. Bob floated above them, clutching the Medal of Honor in his hand.

* * *

Joey's heart began to pound in his chest. He did not see his friends—or Bob—anywhere.

Suddenly, in a quick burst, Barry and Kevin dropped from the sky onto the grass in front of him. He looked up, startled, and saw Bob descending. He landed softly, the medal in his hand.

"Looks like the game is over," Bob said with glee. "And I win!"

Joey helped Barry and Kevin to their feet.

"You stupid idiots," Bob was saying. "You thought it would be so simple, didn't you? You thought this medal would solve all your problems? Well, you were wrong! It didn't help you—just like it didn't help me! The night I died, I clutched this medal in my hand, hoping it would make me braver…stronger! I held it in my hand and screamed inside my head as those bullies broke into my house and taunted me, chased me around, laughed that my dad was dead and my mom sick! And when I tried to run down into the basement, I tripped. I fell all the way down. And by the time I hit the basement floor, I was dead. I tried to be brave and honorable, like my father. AND NOW LOOK AT ME!"

This last bit was punctuated by a crash of thunder. Bob's face was twisted and horrible; he was transforming before their eyes into something from another world. His black eyeholes morphed, his brow growing jagged, permanently embedding anger over his spinning black eyes. His nose grew crooked and long, and his teeth were no longer white, but brown and serrated, like broken glass.

The boys, despite the terror unfolding before them, all exchanged a look of surprise. The newspapers *had* gotten it wrong. After all these decades, finally, someone knew the truth: Bob *hadn't* been murdered. He had died…by accident…running from three lousy bullies.

"This isn't a storybook, or some creep show," Bob roared, his voice different and deeper. "In real life, nothing will save you! And now, time to die!"

"STOP!" boomed an ancient sounding voice. The boys (both living and dead) looked and saw a tall dark figure silhouetted against the night. Lightning flashed, and Joey saw who it was: the old caretaker who had given them such trouble when they had been looking for Bob Smah's grave—seemingly a million years ago.

Bob Smah looked at the caretaker, confusion on his ghostly face. And then there was a look of recognition.

"Ralph," Bob whispered. "Is that you?"

Joey remembered the passage from the journal; the part about one of the bullies being named Ralph.

Ralph Gardner.

"You gotta stop this, Bobby," Ralph said softly, stepping closer to them. "Let these kids go."

Bob snickered. "Like you and your friends let *me* go, Ralph?"

"It was an accident!" Ralph shouted.

"An accident?" Bob said, sounding offended. "You and your stupid friends *killed me*!"

Ralph looked down at his own two feet, then looked back up. There were tears in his sad eyes. "I'm so sorry, kid. I really am. We shouldn't've been so rotten to you. I wish I could take it all back. I wish I had stood up against Tough back then; told'im what a jerk he was. But I was just a stupid kid—we all were. And not a day has gone by that I haven't regretted the part we played in your...death."

Bob shook his head. "It's too little, too late, Ralph."

"They're all dead now, Bobby," Ralph continued. "Tough and Wendell, they're both gone, buried somewhere in this here cemetery. The only one left is me. So if you wanna take your anger out on someone, take it out on me. But not these kids. They only wanted to help you. Let them go."

"I agree with the old guy, Bob!" Kevin cried.

"SHUT UP!" Bob screamed. He swatted his hand in Kevin's direction, and a strong force suddenly hit Kevin square in the chest and he flew backward, crashing against a tombstone.

"Kevin!" Joey cried out. He moved to help his friend, but Bob pointed a finger at him.

"Don't you move!" Bob said.

Ralph took a few steps closer. "Bobby, you need to stop. You gotta move on; leave this world behind."

Bob laughed contemptuously. "Move on, Ralph? Yeah, like it's so easy! Like I can just let go of all the bad things that happened to me!"

Still clutching the medal, he placed it down on top of a tombstone.

"See, it's—"

Bob suddenly froze. His black eyes were fixed on the tombstone. *His* tombstone. He had never seen it before; he had never been anywhere near his grave. His lips quivered as he read his own name carved in the granite. He traced his finger along the lettering. His eyes darted from his name to the stones of his parents. His black eyes rolled over white and took on a human form. He let loose a single choked sob.

In a flash of lightning, Bob saw the translucent figures of his parents suddenly standing by their graves. They looked youthful and vibrant; alive. His father wore his army uniform; his mother's hair was dark and fine. They looked upon him with sympathetic eyes, and stretched out their hands. Their lips did not move—they did not speak; yet Bob heard them all the same.

Come home to us, Bob. We still love you. We never stopped. You don't have to be like this anymore.

"Oh," Bob whimpered. "I'm so sorry."

"Who is he talking to?" Barry yelled over the howling wind. No one answered, for no one saw what Bob was seeing.

Bob stretched out his small hand to the waiting hands of his parents. Their fingers almost touched. A bolt of lightning descended from the heavens and slammed right into the Medal of Honor, which lay on top of the tombstone. A blast of light and sparks exploded from the stone and engulfed Bob. His body was wrapped in bluish light, which traveled around him like living jungle vines.

Joey, Barry, Kevin, and even Ralph, cried out, shielding their eyes as they were all blown backwards, landing hard on their backs.

In the Town Hall steeple, the bell chimed midnight.

364 DAYS TILL HALLOWEEN

CHAPTER TWENTY-NINE

The smoke cleared.

No one spoke.

No one moved.

And then…a groan.

"What happened?" asked Barry, struggling to sit up. The back of his yellow costume was soaked through with muddy cemetery water.

Joey was also woozy from the sudden force that had touched down in the graveyard.

Kevin stood up, shaking and lightly disoriented.

"What was that?" Joey asked his friends. "Did it work?"

Ralph slowly pulled himself up on his shaky legs. "I can't believe what I just saw…"

"Yeah, well, join the club, Mr. Caretaker, sir," Barry said.

"Hey," Kevin groggily said, touching his bare head. "Where's my hat? Anyone see my hat?"

Someone handed Kevin his lucky blue ball cap.

"Oh, thanks," Kevin said.

"You're welcome," said Bob.

Kevin shrieked and backed away, letting the hat fall from his hands.

The boys all shouted in alarm. Ralph took a step forward, as if to shield the boys.

"Guys..." Joey began, his voice dripping with apologetic fear. "Guys, I'm sorry—it didn't work."

Barry yelped and leapt behind Joey and Kevin, cowering.

"Bobby, don't!" Ralph cried out.

Bob looked at all of them curiously. And then he said, "Thank you."

His appearance was free of the horrible features that had plagued the boys' walking nightmares. His black eyes were gone. His broken-glass teeth and his peeling, rotten features. The demonic anger.

Gone.

He now appeared as he had in one of the many photos the boys had seen with their own eyes in the house on Creep Street. A single tear rolled down Bob's cheek.

"Are you...okay?" asked Barry, unsure of how to even phrase the question.

"Of course he's not!" said Kevin. "He's a ghost—an EVIL ghost! We gotta stop him!"

"Wait!" Joey said, blocking Kevin's advance with a single arm.

"But I *am* okay," Bob said, calmly. "I wasn't okay for a long, long time. But I am now."

Ralph dropped down onto his knees and suddenly began to sob into his weathered hands. Bob took a step closer, and placed a hand on Ralph's shoulder.

"I'm so sorry," Ralph wept. "I'm so sorry..."

"It's okay," Bob said softly. "I forgive you."

Ralph looked up at Bob with wet eyes, and it looked as if twenty years had suddenly been lifted from the old man's wrinkled face.

The sky began to slowly illuminate—whatever storm clouds had gathered were slowly dissolving, overtaken by the bright white. At first they thought it was the sun breaking through and welcoming the following day. But it wasn't the sun. It was something else—something unnatural, yet beautiful. Reassuring. Warm.

Bob shook his head, and even smiled. A normal, boyish smile. This sight strangely reassured Joey—it reminded him of when he'd grown attached to a character in a book and felt strongly protective of him. At that moment, Bob was that character—a boy who for all intents and purposes did not exist...but did.

The swirling white cascaded across the night sky, and what could only be described as a tornado—but spinning slowly and softly—descended from the sky. It touched down on the wet cemetery ground, just over Bob's grave.

"You saved me," Bob said.

Joey smiled—a sad but grateful smile.

"Thank you," Bob said, and he stepped backwards into the swirling white light—his salvation. "Thank you, all."

And with that, he became lost in the enclosure of swirling white that swept him off the ground and into the dazzling sky. The white light—and Bob—instantly vanished. Gone. Like when the power snaps off during a heavy rainstorm.

The boys did not speak for several moments. Ralph, still on his knees, slowly got up onto his feet, with a little help from the boys.

"He's okay, then?" Barry asked hopefully. "What we all just saw—that was a good thing, right?"

Joey nodded. He was surer of it than anything. "He's fine. He's where he belongs."

"You boys best get out of here," Ralph said. "I imagine your folks are worried, you bein' out so late and all."

Kevin checked his empty wrists, and not seeing a watch, grabbed Joey's docile arm and whipped it up. "Holy smokes!" he cried. "It's after midnight! We gotta get home!"

Joey finally snapped out of whatever it was he was feeling and realized Kevin was right. Redemption of a spirit—that's one thing. An angry Mr. Tonelli? That's a whole other problem!

The boys dashed to their scattered bikes.

"Wait, the medal," said Kevin and went to grab it from Bob's tombstone. "What should we do with it?"

Joey thought for a moment and then dropped to his knees. He took the medal from Kevin and hand-dug a small hole over Bob's grave. He dropped the medal in and then smoothed the dirt back over the hole.

The boys made their way to the gate. Joey looked back over his shoulder and saw Ralph standing by the Smah graves. The old man raised his hand slowly, in a gesture of farewell.

"Joey, c'mon!" Barry yelled, and the boys fled from the cemetery, home to their angry and worried parents, and to the realization that they had accomplished something most other people never would. They had reunited a family…separated not by miles, but death.

The boys felt like heroes.

Because they were.

CHAPTER THIRTY

They rode their bikes in silence through the empty, wet streets. The rain had stopped, the clouds had parted, and there was a cool breeze. The town slept. Houses dark; jack-o-lanterns extinguished; wet toilet paper hung from trees.

They skidded their bikes to a stop at the beginning of Kevin's street.

"Well…" Kevin said quietly.

"Well…" Joey said.

"I know, right?" Barry joined in.

Then they all cracked up. They had no control over it. The long night had taken its toll on them, exhausted them to giddiness, and the three friends laughed themselves silly.

"So," Joey sarcastically began, "the next time I suggest we go trick-or-treating, how about you guys just *do it?*"

They laughed again.

"See you guys tomorrow," Kevin said.

"See ya, Kevin," Barry said.

"See ya, man," Joey said, smiling.

"'It's been a pleasure working with you, Dr. Venkman,'" Kevin quoted, and rode his bike off into the night, the darkness of his street swallowing him up.

Barry and Joey rode on.

"My dad's probably gonna kill me," Joey said. "But it was worth it."

"Yeah," Barry said. "It was. Except for the rats."

As they turned onto their street, Joey was suddenly filled with dread. The porch light of his house was still on, and he could see the shadowy figure of a man standing there.

"Uh oh," Joey muttered.

"I guess I'll leave you to it," Barry said. "See you in school tomorrow?"

"Holy crap," Joey said. "I forgot it was a school night."

"Maybe our parents will let us stay home," Barry offered.

"Yeah, because we'll be in the hospital recovering from our beatings."

"See ya, Joey," Barry said with a wry smile and pedaled home.

Joey pulled up in front of his house and was startled to see it wasn't Dad on the porch.

It was Michael.

"Michael!" Joey said. "Where's Dad? Is he out looking for me…to kill?"

"No," Michael laughed softly. "He's inside throwing out our empties. We drank…a lot of beers, Joey. I mean, a lot. I'm surprised I can still walk—"

"Michael, you won't believe what happened tonight!" Joey cried. "We *fought* the ghost of Bob Smah! And we saved his soul! And a dog bit my neck open but it wasn't a real dog and we went into the house and—"

"Slow down there, buddy," Michael laughed. "I think you should keep these…crazy stories to yourself."

"But—"

"Look, I better go," Michael said. "Your dad will be right back out."

"Is he mad?"

"You'll have to ask him that," Michael said, and started to walk down the street.

"Hey!" Joey called. "That amulet you sold us was a fake! It didn't work!"

Michael turned and smiled. "Of course it didn't," he said. "There's no such thing as ghosts."

He turned and walked away, whistling down the block.

Joey was about to creep inside, with hopes of getting in bed unnoticed, when the door opened and his father stepped out. He looked down at Joey, who looked up, gulping.

"Hi, sir," Joey managed, weakly.

"Out awfully late, Joey," Dad said in a stern voice.

"I…I'm sorry…it's just that—"

"Forget it," Dad sighed. "Look, I'm sorry I got so mad at you. Michael reminded me that I was your age once…I think. And I did stupid things, too. I just want you to be safe, that's all."

"Dad, remember when I asked you for advice about someone, and I told you when it was over I would tell you all about it?" Joey asked. "Well, I want to tell you. You see—"

"Don't worry about it," Dad said. "It's okay. I trust you. You may be obsessed with stupid monster movies and rubber skeletons, but you're a good kid, Joey."

Joey blushed and looked down at his sneakers. "Does Mom know I was out so late?" he whispered.

"No way," Dad laughed. "She went to bed. And let's not tell her, or she'll throw us both in the garbage can."

"Okay," Joey said. "Dad?"

"Son?"

"Can I stay home from school tomorrow?"

"Don't push your luck. Go to bed."

Joey trudged up the steps onto the porch, his head down. Dad reached out to give him a hug, and then reconsidered. He patted Joey on the shoulder instead.

"Oh, fine," he said and looked at his son's face, which was smeared with black and gray make-up. "You can stay home tomorrow. Now go wash up, you look like one of my co-workers."

Joey smiled, exhausted, and went upstairs, his body aching. He washed, changed, and practically collapsed into bed—asleep before he hit the pillow.

Halloween was officially over.

And the three friends would never forget it .

CHAPTER THIRTY-ONE

It was mid-afternoon, and Joey had been lying on his bed for most of the day thinking about Bob Smah. The experience had been so many things: terrifying, saddening, and rewarding. He wondered if he would ever have another one like it.

The phone rang, but Joey ignored it—he was too deep in thought. The ringing ceased, and Mom almost immediately called to him.

"Joey!" said Mom from the bottom of the stairs. "It's your little friend, Barry!"

Joey reached lazily for the phone on his nightstand and picked it up. "I got it!" he shouted to his mother and waited for her to hang up.

"What's up, Barrman?" Joey said.

"Have you seen today's paper?" Barry said on the other end of the phone.

"No, I guess I forgot to check my stocks!" Joey said, laughing and rolling his eyes.

"Go grab it. I'll wait."

Joey ran downstairs and grabbed *The Blackwood Blackboard* off the kitchen table, then ran back upstairs to his room. There was a headline on the front page that read **DOG SAVES CAT FROM HOUSE FIRE!**

"What, the dog story?" Joey said. "Neat, I guess."

"No, turn to the obituaries," Barry said.

"Oh man, I think I've had enough death for a while," Joey said.

"Do it," Barry said urgently.

Joey flipped to the obituaries, his eyes scanning the black and white print.

"What am I looking for?" he said.

"You'll know when you see it."

And he did: near the bottom of the page was the name RALPH GARDNER.

Joey read on:

Ralph Gardner, aged 83, passed away suddenly on the evening of October 30. Gardner had been the gravedigger, and then caretaker, at Resurrection Cemetery for almost sixty years. He lived in Blackwood for his entire life.

"Wow," Joey said. "I guess everything that happened last night was too much for him…"

"Joey, look again—look at *when* he died," Barry said.

Joey looked at the obituary again, and this time he caught it: the evening of October *30th*.

That meant Ralph was dead when he confronted Bob Smah in the cemetery!

"Holy smokes!" Joey cried.

"Bob Smah wasn't the *only* ghost we saw last night," Barry said.

"I guess Ralph had his own unfinished business to stick around for," Joey said.

"It's a shame," Barry said. "When he wasn't being terrifying, he seemed like nice man."

"But at least he finally got to tell Bob he was sorry," Joey said, folding the paper.

"Yeah," Barry agreed.

"So, are you okay? I mean, after everything—"

"Well, considering we're not ghost food, I think I'm fine," Barry said, laughing.

"You guys were really great last night," Joey said. "Both of you were super brave."

"Well, maybe Kevin was..." Barry said bashfully.

"No, you were, too. And I really am sorry for all the times Kevin and I made fun of your weight. We weren't trying to be—"

"Joey, it's okay, really," Barry said. "I understand. Besides, if this phone call gets any more mushy, we're going to have to start using the girls' room at school."

Joey laughed.

"I'll talk to you later," Barry said.

The boys hung up. Joey was about to bring the newspaper back downstairs so his father could read *Pickle-Eater,* his favorite comic strip, when the phone rang again. He answered it.

"You really convinced your dad to let you stay home today?" Kevin asked with disbelief.

"Yeah, can you believe it?"

"I can't! I expected to receive the invitation to your funeral today."

The boys laughed.

"Have you been thinking about it all day?" asked Kevin. "About Bob?"

"I have," Joey admitted.

"Me, too. I don't think I heard a single thing in school today. I just stared forward and replayed the whole thing over and over. Then I realized that I had to come home and call you so I could tell you something."

"What?" Joey asked.

"That I'm sorry," Kevin said, without hesitation. "I was a jerk to you during the whole thing. You can't blame me for not having believed it right away, but I didn't have to be so lame about it."

"Don't worry about it," Joey said dismissively. "It's not important."

"I just wanted you to know that…it's not like I didn't trust you or anything. It was just hard to swallow at first, you know? Ghosts and haunted houses…it was weird."

Joey heard a sound outside and it piqued his curiosity. Kevin continued his apology, but Joey was only half listening as he crept to his window.

"…you like horror movies and comic books, and I just assumed you were overreact…"

Joey moved his curtain aside and peered down into the dark street. Across the street was the former Winslow house—recently sold and apparently now home to someone new. A small moving truck was parked in front of the house, and a utility van—like the one his dad drove—was parked in the driveway.

"…and meeting Michael was just…that guy was so weird! With his pet bird and…"

Joey watched as an older man reached into his van and withdrew a small crate. Joey recognized the crate from the times they had taken their dog, Max, to the vet. They were animal carriers, and judging from the size, they were probably for cats. The man retrieved one animal carrier after another from his van and walked them into his house. Two at a time. Joey counted ten trips into the house...

Does this weird dude really have twenty cats? What is he doing with so many?

"...even after everything that happened, I'm glad we did it, and as crazy as it sounds, I would probably do it again," Kevin finished.

"What was that last part?" Joey asked, snapping back to reality.

"I said I would probably do it again," Kevin repeated.

"I'm glad to hear you say that," Joey said, his one hand still holding back his curtain, eyes still warily on his new neighbor—his new neighbor with the twenty cats.

"Why?" Kevin asked.

"Because I'm watching my new neighbor move in...and he is definitely suspicious looking."

"Oh, no," Kevin moaned. "Forget I said anything."

"No, really," Joey said. "This guy...there's something not right about him."

"Joey, no!" Kevin said.

"Hey, listen, we should start doing this all the time!" Joey said emphatically. "Investigating the strange things that go on in our neighborhood! It could be, like, our thing!"

"La la la!" Kevin sang sarcastically over the phone, drowning out Joey's ramblings.

"I'm serious!" Joey said. "We could even have a name! We could call ourselves The Fright Fr—"

Kevin hung up.

"Kevin!" Joey shouted into the dead phone and muttered. "Thanks for nothing, dude!"

He hung up the phone and looked back out the window. The van was locked up now. The house was dark...except for a single room: the basement. Flashing and pulsating light shone through the window, almost as if there were someone behind it working with strange equipment.

"You're up to something, aren't you, neighbor?" Joey asked. "I believe you are. And I—I mean, WE—are going to find out what. Because that's what we do. Because we are The Fright Fr—"

"JOEY, IT'S DINNER TIME!" Dad bellowed up the stairs. "AND BRING ME THAT *PICKLE-EATER* COMIC!"

"Jeeze!" Joey said. He looked out his window a moment longer before going downstairs to join his family around the dinner table.

ACKNOWLEDGMENTS

The House on Creep Street exists in a world between fantasy and reality. The setting of this adventure—the town of Blackwood—is a real town from which our authors hail, as do the very real people on whom the characters of Joey, Kevin, Barry, and the entire Tonelli family, are based. Make no mistake: they exist even today. And in the town of Blackwood, they lived, and worked, and laughed, and made memories. Their characters' interpretations contained within these pages are based on fond remembrances, made bigger than life through a haze of childhood recollection. Much of these characters' personalities was created, expanded upon, and embellished. Other characters are spawned solely from the imaginations of the authors. You'll have to guess who.

The importance of the real Kevin and Barry, and the real Tonelli family (pseudonym), can never be overstated. It is because of them that we are here, embarking on this journey draped in childhood nostalgia, the comfort of familiar neighborhood streets, and of nighttime adventure. This book is a product of lives spent with friends and family, whose undying support, devotion, and good-natured humoring has led to this very first adventure with The Fright Friends.

The authors wish to acknowledge the real Kevin and Barry, who may not have hunted ghosts in the darkness, but who were instrumental in the foundation of idyllic childhood friendship. The authors extend their never-ending love, thanks, and appreciation.

In addition, the authors acknowledge: Drew Falchetta, artist and illustrator, for the amazing cover art; Carol Ford for her editorial assistance and support; Emily Ambash, for reading the book over and over and repeatedly pointing out how many times the authors mispelled "ghost"; Lina Paola, for her zero-hour hawk-eye edits; Dakota Hampton, The Fright Friends' very first reader and fan; and Michael Aloisi, for enabling us to share this adventure with you all.

Lastly, the authors thank the real Bob Smah. May he rest in peace...

ABOUT THE AUTHORS

Edgar and Allan Blood were both October-born and subsequently abandoned in the woods. After being raised by wolves, the brothers set out on a worldwide journey to find their fortune, until they were separated by a brutal snow-thunder-hurricane, which left them believing each other to be dead. They were reunited under the most amazing and unbelievable circumstances—but that's another story. Together again, the brothers honed their literary skills through jobs writing obituaries and ransom notes. To tell them apart, remember: Edgar has an eye patch and Allan has a wooden leg—but sometimes it's the other way around. When the Blood Brothers are not writing stories, they work as door-to-door coffin salesmen.

Visit www.TheFrightFriends.com for additional ghoulery.

CPSIA information can be obtained
at www.ICGtesting.com
Printed in the USA
FFOW03n1553281014
8365FF